FAVORITE YIDDISH STORIES

FAVORITE YIDDISH STORIES

Edited by
IRVING HOWE
and
ELIEZER GREENBERG

WINGS BOOKS
New York • Avenel, New Jersey

Grateful acknowledgment is made for permission to use the following:
"The Conjuror" by I.L. Peretz, translated by Joachim Neugroshel from *The Great Works of Jewish Fantasy and Occult*, is reprinted by permission from the Overlook Press. English translation copyright © 1976 by Joachim Neugroshel. Published by the Overlook Press, Woodstock, NY 12498.

"Hanukah Money" from *The Old Country* by Sholom Aleichem. Translated by Frances and Julius Butwin. Copyright (c) 1946, 1974 by Crown Publishers, Inc. Reprinted by permission of Crown Publishers, Inc.

"A Musician Dies" by I.L. Peretz, translated by Nathan Halper. From *Selected Stories* by I.L. Peretz, edited by Irving Howe and Eliezer Greenberg. Copyright (c) 1974 by Schocken Books Inc. Reprinted by permission of Schocken Books, published by Pantheon Books, a division of Random House, Inc.

"The Oath", "The Purim Gift" and "Reb Asher the Dairyman" from In *My Father's Court* by Isaac Bashevis Singer. Copyright (c) 1963, 1966 by Isaac Bashevis Singer. Reprinted by permission of Farrar, Straus & Giroux, Inc.

"On Account of a Hat" by Sholom Aleichem, trans. by Isaac Rosenfeld, "The Adventures of Hershel Summerwind" by Itzik Manger, trans. Irving Howe, from *A Treasury of Yiddish Stories* by Irving Howe and Eliezer Greenberg. Copyright (c) 1953, 1954, 1989 by Viking Penguin, renewed (c) 1981, 1982 by Irving Howe and Eva Greenberg. Used by permission of Viking Penguin, a division of Penguin Books USA, Inc.

"Rabchik, A Jewish Dog," by Sholom Aleichem, reprinted by permission of the Family of Sholom Aleichem.

Originally published as *Yiddish Stories Old & New*
Copyright (c) 1974 by Irving Howe and Eliezer Greenberg
All rights reserved.
This 1992 edition is published by Wings Books, distributed by Outlet Book Company, Inc., a Random House Company, 40 Engelhard Avenue, Avenel, New Jersey, 07001, by arrangement with Irving Howe and the estate of Eliezer Greenberg.

Printed and bound in the United States of America

Library of Congress Cataloging-in-Publication Data

Yiddish stories, old and new.
    Favorite Yiddish stories / edited by Irving Howe and Eliezer Greenberg.
        p. cm.
    Originally published: Yiddish stories, old and new. New York: Holiday House, © 1974
    Contents: About the stories — Hanukah money / by Sholom Aleichem — Rabchik, a Jewish dog / by Sholom Aleichem — On account of a hat / by Sholom Aleichem — The conjuror / by I.L. Peretz — A musician dies / by I.L. Peretz — Iron / by Abraham Reisen — The last of the line / by I.D. Berkowitz—White feet / by Isaac Metzker — The oath / by Isaac Bashevis Singer — The purim gift / by Isaac Bashevis Singer — Reb Asher the dairyman / by Isaac Bashevis Singer — The adventures of Hershel Summerwind / by Itzik Manger — The machine / by Joseph Opatoshu — Blossoms / by Isaiah Spiegel.
    ISBN 0-517-06656-4
    1. Jews — Europe, Eastern — Juvenile fiction. 2. Short stories, Yiddish —
Translations into English.
    [1. Jews — Europe, Eastern — Fiction. 2. Short stories.] I. Howe, Irving II. Greenberg, Eliezer,
1896- . III. Title.
PZ5.F27555   1992
[Fic] — dc20

                                                                    91-33047
                                                                          CIP
8 7 6 5 4 3 2 1

Contents

CONTENTS

About the Stories

Almost all the stories in this book are about Jews in eastern Europe during the late nineteenth and early twentieth centuries. Millions of Jews lived there at that time, most of them in Russia and Poland, but many others in Rumania, Austria-Hungary, and Lithuania.

Their living conditions were usually very bad. In Russia, for example, harsh laws prohibited Jews from entering certain cities, from owning land, and from attending schools and universities freely. Earning a living was often a desperate problem, and much of Yiddish literature deals with the tragi-comic strategies that the Jews had to employ in order to feed their families. Sometimes they were the victims of pogroms, or semi-organized riots, in which the Russian peasants, stirred up by evil-spirited governmental authorities, would beat Jews and damage their homes and stores. In short, life was always dangerous and difficult. It was marked by hardships that few of us are likely to have experienced directly. Yet, despite all these troubles, the Jews of eastern Europe built up a rich culture, a way of life that seemed to them full of spiritual meaning and beauty, sometimes even personal joy.

The language these Jews spoke was Yiddish, and all the stories in this book have been translated from the Yiddish. It is a language that uses the Hebrew alphabet, and it has borrowed, over the centuries, a fair portion of its vocabulary from Hebrew. First arising in the Rhine region of Germany about a thousand years ago, Yiddish has also freely taken words from many other European languages, including German, Russian, Provençal, and English. But with time it became a distinct language of its own, full of crackling vividness and sparkle. In the life of the east European Jews, Yiddish was the language of daily speech, while Hebrew continued to be used, as it had been by the Jews for thousands of years, as the language of prayer and religious learning. Yiddish was the language of the ordinary week, Hebrew the language of the radiant Sabbath. Everyone knew Yiddish, and most people had a smattering of Hebrew.

Outwardly poor and wretched, the community of the east European Jews was spiritually ablaze. What it valued most was religious learning and meditation. For these Jews, God was a living presence, an immediate force, a voice that spoke to them. To worship God and to study the sacred texts, to give one's life not to wealth or power in this world but to communion with holiness— this seemed to the east European Jews the great purpose of human existence. Not, of course, that all or even many of them were able to achieve this purpose; but almost all of them honored and revered those Jews who tried to.

The remarkable sense of intimacy with God, which flourished among the east European Jews, enabled them to endure all kinds of suffering. It persuaded them that life had value and significance; it gave them courage to accept humiliation and face martyrdom; it created an aura of beauty around their ramshackle synagogues, their bare little houses, their isolated villages. And because they felt so close to God, they could often speak to him with a personal familiarity, even a critical impatience, that might shock people of other faiths. A good part of Yiddish humor makes fun of the contrast between this sense of religious exaltation, on the one hand, and the painful circumstances of daily Jewish life, on the other.

By the middle of the nineteenth century, if not somewhat earlier, the religious unity of the east European Jewish world had been shattered. Modern ideas—individualism, disbelief in God, a new concern with science, hopes for personal freedom—had begun to reach the east European Jews. Some of them wanted to adapt their religion to the new circumstances of European life. Others, still a small minority, wanted to abandon religion altogether. Some Jews felt it was time to rebel against the miserable life to which they had submitted for centuries, and strong socialist and Zionist movements arose among them toward the end of the nineteenth century. By then, also, large numbers of Jews came to the conclusion that there was no future for them in eastern Europe and that they would have to find a new place in which to live. There began, then, the great historical journey to America.

By the time most of the Yiddish story writers started to do their work—that is, by about 1890 or 1900 —the world of the east European Jews had lost its traditional stability. Yet even those who rebelled against the old ways still remained emotionally attached to them. Children, for example, still received orthodox religious educations in the Talmud Torah, or Hebrew school, and they were still expected to continue along the pathways of religion.

It was a world in which the life of children was often hard, even harsh: long hours in the Hebrew schools, severe poverty at home, the absence of many of the little pleasures that we take for granted. Yet they still found ways to amuse themselves, to have fun, and to create mischief.

In the very close family life of the east European Jews, children were often treated with great affection, even indulgence. For through their love of children the Jews released emotions of tenderness for which they often had no other outlet. Through their love of children they signaled to themselves and to the future the kind of warm-hearted life they would have wanted to lead if only circumstances had made it possible.

THE EDITORS

SHOLOM ALEICHEM

Hanukah Money

It is a traditional Jewish custom that on Hanukah, the holiday that celebrates the victory of the Maccabees over the Romans, grownups are expected to give gifts of money to children, and children are then free to spend that money in any way they wish. You can imagine that Jewish children looked forward with great eagerness to this holiday. In Hanukah Money, Sholom Aleichem describes both the inner warmth of Jewish family life during the celebration of this holiday and the glee and excitement felt by two brothers as they reckon their gifts.

Which of the holidays is best?

Hanukah! Eight whole days with no school. Potato pancakes to eat; a *dreidl* or top, to spin; and Hanukah money comes from every side. Who needs a better holiday?

Winter! It's cold out. A burning frost. Danger. The windows are tightly closed, streaked and decorated with snow in the finest way. Inside, a warmth to delight the soul.

The silver candle-holder for Hanukah has been ready since morning. Father paces the room, his hands clasped behind his back, praying the evening prayers. When he's done, he takes a wax candle—the first candle —from a drawer and says to us, to me and my younger brother Motl, "Call your mother to the blessing of the Hanukah lights."

My brother Motl and I dash off, tumbling over each other. "Mamma, quick. Hanukah lights."

In the kitchen, Mother throws her work aside (melting goose fat and baking potato pancakes) and runs to the living room. Behind her is Breinah the cook, a dark woman with a moustache, a fat face, and hands that are always greasy. Mother stands to one side and makes a pious face. At the door, Breinah the cook wipes her hands in her dirty apron, makes a swipe at her nose with a pudgy hand, and leaves a black smudge across her whole face. We have to be made of iron— my brother Motl and I—to keep from exploding with laughter.

Father goes to the candleholder, the lighted first candle in his hand, bows his head and chants the familiar melody of the blessing. Mother answers, "Amen," and Breinah the cook nods her head, at the same time making such faces that my brother and I are afraid to look at one another.

Father watches the Hanukah lights and wanders, praying, around the room. He prays and prays and never stops praying. We are eager to see an end to it. We want him to reach in his pocket for his wallet.

My brother and I make signals and poke each

other. "Motl, you go. Ask for Hanukah money."

"Why me? Why should *I*?"

"Because you're the younger. That's why."

"You've got it wrong. You're older. You're the one who should ask for it."

Father knows very well we're talking about Hanukah money, but he pretends not to hear. Quietly, without hurry, he starts counting money. We feel shivery all over. Our hands tremble; our hearts beat faster. We stare at the ceiling, scratch our heads, and pretend to be calm—as if it had nothing to do with us.

Father coughs, "Hrrrm. Hrrrm. Children, come here."

"Huh? Whh . . . what?"

"Here. Hanukah money."

The money in our fists, we start to walk away, my brother Motl and I. At first, slowly, like well-behaved boys, then a little faster and faster; then springing and leaping until, arrived at our room, we can no longer contain ourselves and make triple somersaults and cartwheels, hopping and dancing and singing:

> *Engeh, Bengeh,*
> *Stupeh Tsenyeh,*
> *Artseh, Bartseh,*
> *Goleh, Schvartseh,*
> *Aimeleh, reimeleh,*
> *Beigeleh, feigeleh,*
> *Hup.*

And we exchange slaps for sheer joy.

The door opens and Uncle Benny comes in. "Hey, gang. You've got Hanukah money coming to you."

Uncle Benny puts his hand into his vest pocket, takes out two silver coins, and gives them to us.

Nobody in the world would ever guess that Father and Uncle Benny are brothers. Father is tall and skinny; Uncle Benny is short and stocky. Father is always worried and silent; Uncle Benny is cheerful and talkative, day and night, summer and winter. Just the same, they are really brothers.

Father takes a sheet of paper and marks it into squares: black squares and white squares. Then he asks for black and white beans from the kitchen to use for checkers.

Mother is in the kitchen, still melting goose fat and baking potato pancakes. My brother Motl and I are spinning our *dreidl.* Father and Uncle Benny sit down to play checkers.

"I want to ask one thing of you, Benny: no tricks and no changes. That means, *a move is a move,*" says Father.

"A move is a move," says Uncle Benny, and makes a move.

"A move is a move," says Father as he jumps Uncle Benny's checker.

The more deeply they settle into their game, the more they chew at their beards, shuffle their feet under the table, and sing softly the same melody. "Oh, what's to be done, to be done, to be done," Father sings with the melody of the *Gemarah,* and chews at the corner of his beard. "If I move here, he'll go there. So . . . I'll go there. If he moves here, then I'd do better to go . . . *that* way."

"That way . . . that way . . . that way," Uncle Benny helps him along, in the same fashion.

"So what's there to be afraid of?" Father sings on.
"If he takes *that* checker from me, I'll take two of his.
But what if he takes three checkers?"

"Three checkers, three checkers, three checkers,"
Uncle Benny sings, encouraging him.

"Oh, you are a fool, Benny. A fool, and a big one,"
Father sings, and makes a move.

"You are a fool yourself, my brother, and a bigger
one," sings Benny as he makes a move which he draws
right back.

"Shame, Benny. We agreed: *a move is a move*,"
Father says, no longer chanting and grabs at Benny's
hand.

"So?" Benny says. "If I'm still in the middle of a
move, I can go wherever I please."

"No," says Father. "We agreed. When you move,
it's finished. We discussed it: no tricks and no changes."

"Changes!" says Uncle Benny, "How often does it
happen that *you* change *your* mind?"

"I?" says Father. "You see Benny, why I hate to
play checkers with you."

"Who forces you to play with me?"

"Already quarreling over a bean?" cries Mother,
coming red-faced out of the kitchen followed by
Breinah carrying a huge platter filled with hot potato
pancakes smeared with goose fat, the steam rising from
them. Everyone goes to the table. My brother Motl
and I, though we had earlier been fighting like cats and
dogs, settle down now to the potato pancakes.

"Well Motl, let's work it out . . . how much Hanukah
money did we get? Now you be quiet. I'll count mine
first. Then you can count yours."

So I count: "A dollar, and three quarters, and four

dimes and five nickels and six pennies. How much is that all together? That looks like . . . a dollar, and three quarters, and four dimes and five nickels and six pennies. . . ."

My brother Motl won't wait till I've finished and starts to count his money. He passes the coins from one hand to the other and counts: "A quarter and a quarter makes two quarters. And another quarter makes three quarters. And two nickels and three quarters is three quarters and two nickels. And a nickel and a nickel? That makes two nickels with three quarters, which makes three quarters and two nickels. Oops! What am I talking about? I'll have to start again."

He starts all over once more. We count and count and can't get the money counted. When we come to Uncle Moshe Aaron's old quarters, worn-out dimes, and grease-swollen nickels, we get so mixed up that we don't know where we are. We try to get the coins exchanged, offering them to Father, to Mother, to Breinah the cook, but no luck. No one will touch them. They ask, "What sort of coins are these? Who gave you this kind of money?"

We keep quiet, ashamed to tell.

At night, in bed, I lie awake, thinking, "How much would I make if all my uncles, and all my aunts, and all my relatives were to give me Hanukah money? First, there's Uncle Abraham Baer, my mother's brother—a cheapskate, but he's rich. Then there's Uncle Itcheh and Aunt Deborah with whom Father and Mother haven't spoken for years. Then what about Uncle Benish and Aunt Yenta? And our sister Aidl? And her husband Sholem-Zaidl? And all the rest of the relatives? . . ."

"Motl, are you asleep?"

"Yes. What is it?"

"How much do you think we'll get from Uncle Moshe Aaron?"

"How should I know? Am I a prophet?"

A minute later: "Motl, are you asleep?"

"Yes, what is it?"

"Does everyone have as many uncles and aunts as we do?"

"Maybe yes; maybe no."

Two minutes later: "Motl, are you asleep?"

"Yes, what is it?"

"If you're asleep, how come you're talking to me?"

"You ask me something, so I answer. . . ."

Three minutes later: "Motl, are you asleep?"

"Zzzzzzzz, hrhrhrhrhr, khn, khn, khn, hrhrhr." Motl snores, snorts, whistles through his nose. I sit up in bed, take out my dollar, pet it, fondle it and think, "What is it? Just a piece of paper. But oh, what it can *buy*— toys, knives, sticks, wallets, candies, raisins, fruit. Who knows what else?"

I put the dollar under my pillow and say my prayers. And there comes Breinah from the kitchen with an entire platterful of dollars. Breinah doesn't walk; she floats through the air. And Motl is swallowing dollars like hot cakes.

With all my might, I cry, "Motl, For heaven's sake, what are you doing? Swallowing dollars?"

I wake up and spit three times against the evil eye. *Ptui, ptui, ptui.* A dream.

And fall asleep.

translated by Leonard Wolf

SHOLOM ALEICHEM

Rabchik, A Jewish Dog

Rabchik is a dog with all the appetites and habits of dogs. But he is also a special kind of dog, a Jewish dog, and it's hard not to feel that the story of Rabchik's troubles has some connection with Jewish woes and miseries, too.

Rabchik was a dog with white spots. Not a big dog—middle-sized—quiet, not a grabber. He did not, as other dogs do, like to jump at one from behind to snatch at a hem or take a bite out of a leg. He was happiest just to be left alone. So it follows that every God-fearing person picked on him. Giving Rabchik a blow with a stick, or kicking him when his back was turned, or throwing a rock at his head, or emptying a slop-pail at him, was sport for everyone—almost a pious duty. Rabchik, attacked this way, did not, as other dogs might, pause to discuss the matter or bark his distress, or show his teeth. No. After receiving his blows, Rabchik would grovel, belly nearly to the ground, and whine: "*Aie, aie, aie.*" Then, his tail between his legs, he would run off to hide in some corner where he sank into deep thought and snapped at flies.

Who was Rabchik? Where did he come from? That's hard to know. It may be that he was left behind by the former landlord of the yard. It may be that he missed his way, lost his owner, adopted a new one and stayed on. You know how such things happen: one is taking a walk, and then—there's a lost dog in your tracks. You think, "Hey, what's this tagging along?" You raise your hand to the dog and shout, "Beat it!" The dog stops, bows like a human, and just as you're trying to smack him one, manages to get even closer. Now you bend; you make a feint with your hand, pretending to throw a rock at him. It does no good. You stand watching the dog; the dog stands watching you. You look silently into each other's eyes. You spit, and start off again. The dog follows, and you're going out of your mind. You grab a stick and go at him fiercely, which gives the dog an idea: he lies down, sticks his feet in the air, trembles and shivers and gazes into your eyes as if to say, "Well, you want to beat me? Beat away."
That's the kind of dog our Rabchik was.

Rabchik was not one to snatch at food. You could leave the finest things lying around the house and he would not touch them. He understood clearly that whatever was put *under* the table was meant for him. Anything else was none of his business—though it was said that Rabchik, as a youngster, had been something of a brat. One time, the story goes, as he stalked the meat-salting board, meaning to steal the leg of a goose, he was seen by Breinah the cook, who set up a dreadful racket, crying, "Isaac, Isaac!" Isaac, the handyman, came running in just at the moment when Rabchik was trying to make off with the stolen goose leg. Isaac managed to squeeze Rabchik in the doorway so that Rabchik's front end was on one side of the door, and his hind end on the other. Oh, they really made Rabchik pay: on one side of the door, Isaac banged away at his head with a stick, while on the other side, Breinah beat at him with a chunk of wood, screaming all the while, "Isaac, Isaac!"

That incident left its mark on him. The minute anyone went up to him, looked into his face and said, "Isaac, Isaac," he ran off wherever his legs would take him.

Paraska bothered Rabchik more than anyone. Paraska was the one who did our laundry, whitewashed the walls, and milked the cows. What did she have against Rabchik? It's hard to say, but he annoyed her on sight. The moment she saw him, she was inflamed: "A plague on you, you scurvy hound." And Rabchik, as if on purpose, was invariably under her feet. Paraska, as she worked, avenged herself on him as we do on *Haman*. If she was washing clothes, she would pour a basin of cold water over him. Rabchik hated such a bath, after which he had to shake himself long and hard. If she was whitewashing the walls, she would spatter his face so that he had to lick at himself for an hour at a stretch to get clean. If she was milking the cow, she would throw a chunk of wood at his legs.

Rabchik learned to leap. When he saw a chunk coming his way, he learned to dodge like an elf. There was one time when Rabchik got the worst of such attentions. Paraska had flung a piece of wood which struck his front paw with such force it made him cry out strangely, "*Aie, aie, aie.*" Everyone in the courtyard came running. No sooner did Rabchik see that people were gathering than he began to whimper, showing everyone his broken foot, as if to say, "See, see what Paraska has done," thinking, evidently that they would take his side and that Paraska would be blamed. Perhaps he expected that they would decapitate her for what she had done.

Actually, what happened was that everyone burst out laughing. Moustached Breinah flew out of her kitchen with a big spoon in her hands. Wiping her nose with her bare elbow, she said, "Did they break his stupid foot? Good. Good." As for the street urchins, those delinquents came running from all sides, yelling and whistling, after which Paraska came up and really let him have it, pouring a pitcherful of scalding water over his back. Rabchik howled and yammered, "*Aie, aie, aie,*" as he leaped and twirled, biting his own tail, all the while keeping up such a racket that it excited the youngsters to further laughter. The sight of Rabchik dancing on three legs seemed to unleash their pent-up ugliness, and they went at him with sticks. Rabchik ran off, howling, stumbling, followed by the street boys with their sticks and their stones, whistling and hooting, driving him farther and farther out of the village and beyond the mill.

Rabchik ran on, convinced that he would never come back to the village. He was off, into the wide world, anywhere at all that his legs would carry him. He ran . . . and ran . . . until he reached the next village where he was met by the local dogs. They sniffed him up and down and said, "Welcome, dog. Where are you from? And what sort of decoration is that on your back? It looks as if someone had singed a hunk of hide in the middle of your back."

"Ah, don't ask," says Rabchik sadly. "There's a lot to tell but little worth hearing. Can I spend the night here?"

"With the greatest pleasure," the local dogs say. "The outdoors is roomy enough, and it's even more spacious under the sky."

"What do you do for food?" asks Rabchik. "How do you ease your hungry stomach when it makes its demands?"

"Not bad. Slops can be found everywhere. As for meat—well, God created bones. If the householders eat meat, we get bones. One way or another, our stomachs are filled."

"And your householders? How are they?" asks Rabchik, making an inquiring gesture with his tail.

"The householders are . . . householders," say the dogs, making an end of the matter.

"Well. And . . . Paraska?" Rabchik inquires.

"Paraska? What Paraska?" reply the dogs.

"The Paraska who does the laundry, whitewashes the walls, and milks the cow. You don't know Paraska?"

The village dogs study Rabchik as if he has lost his mind. "What kind of Paraska-stuff is this?" Again, they sniff him over from every side and one by one they drift away, each to his personal garbage heap.

Rabchik thinks, "What fortunate dogs," and stretches out on God's earth, under God's sky, thinking to doze a bit. But he can't sleep. First, there is the matter of his scalded hide; it bites and smarts terribly; and the tormenting flies—no way to drive them off. Second, his stomach is growling. He would like to gnaw on something, but there is nothing to chew. He'll have to wait until morning. And third, he can't sleep because of all the things he heard from the village dogs. There were no Isaacs among them to squeeze him with a door and bang him with a hunk of wood; there were no Paraskas to scald him with boiling water; there were no street boys to whistle at him or beat him with sticks or chase him. There were fortunate dogs in the world! "And I thought my world was the whole world. Well, a worm in horseradish can't imagine anything sweeter."

Rabchik falls asleep and dreams of a huge, brim-full slop-bucket with bread and plenty of tripes and meat scraps, groats, and a mixture of millet and beans. And bones! A whole treasurehouse of bones. Shin bones, rib bones, marrow bones. Fish bones—whole fish-heads waiting to be sucked. Rabchik doesn't know where to begin. The village dogs standing respectfully by say, "Blessed are those who partake," and watch him prepare for his feast.

For politeness sake, Rabchik says, "Come. Eat."

"Eat in good health," say the village dogs in a friendly way.

Suddenly, he hears a voice in his ear crying, "Isaac!"

Rabchik starts up. It was only a dream.

In the morning, Rabchik prowls the yards looking for a slop-kettle, a piece of zwieback, a bit of bone, but wherever he goes, the garbage heaps are taken. "Can one get a bite here?" Rabchik asks.

"You? No. Maybe in the next yard."

Rabchik trots about from yard to yard—everywhere, the same tune. He thinks the matter over and decides that politeness doesn't pay. Much better to make a grab at whatever offers, but at the very first "grab," the local dogs really let him have it. First, they glare at him; then they show their teeth. Then several of them jump him, biting and tearing, ruining his tail; after which they give him an honorable send-off well beyond the village gates.

His tail between his legs, Rabchik starts off to the next village. Arrived there, it is the same story all over again. First, pleasant words; treated like a guest; but the moment he approaches a slop-bucket, there are angry looks, growls, bared teeth, then tearing and biting and "Beat it!" from all sides.

Finally, this prowling from place to place disgusts him and he decides that people are no good, and dogs not much of an improvement. Better to live in the forest among the beasts.

So Rabchik went off to the forest and wandered there alone. One day, two, then three, until he felt his guts shriveling and his stomach cramping more tightly the farther he walked. In the last throes of hunger and thirst, he felt there was nothing left for him but to lie down in mid-forest and perish. It was an annoying thought, because what he wanted most to do was to live.

Tucking his tail under him, Rabchik stretches out his front paws, puts out his tongue, and settles down under a tree to think a dog's thought: "Where to find a bit of bread, a morsel of meat, even a bone, a drop of water?" Thus anguish makes a seeker of him, a philosopher. And he speculates, wondering why he, a dog, is being punished rather than the beasts or the birds or the rest of the world's creatures. For instance, the bird that flies to its nest, or the lizard scurrying home to its hole, or the crawling worm, or the beetle or the ant—they all have their homes and can provide for themselves. "Only I, a dog . . . *bark, bark, bark.*"

"Who barks in the forest?" inquires a hungry wolf, his tongue lolling as he runs.

Rabchik, who has never seen a wolf before, thinks it is a dog. Slowly, he gets to his feet, stretches and approaches the wolf: "Who are you?" the wolf asks arrogantly. "Where are you from, and what are you doing here?"

Rabchik is delighted to have met such a friendly brother, someone to whom he can at least tell his troubles, and he pours out his bitter heart to the wolf. "I'll tell you the truth," says Rabchik, after reciting his list of woes, "I would be just as glad now to meet with a lion or a bear, or even a wolf."

"What would happen, do you suppose?" asks the wolf with a sinister smile.

"Nothing," says Rabchik, "but if I'm destined to die, I'd just as soon a wolf killed me rather than die of hunger among my own kind—among dogs."

"In that case," says the wolf, breathing hard and clicking its teeth, "you should know that *I* am a wolf, and I have a great urge to tear you to bits and make a meal of you. Because I'm terribly hungry. Eight days have gone by since I've had anything to eat."

At these words, Rabchik was so frightened that his singed skin began to tremble. "My lord king, O reverend wolf," Rabchik said tearfully, making a pitiful face, "may God send you a better meal. What will you get eating me? Hide and bones, as you can see. Take my advice, take pity on my dog's bones and let me be."

With that, Rabchik tucked in his tail, arched his back, crawled on his belly and made such ugly gestures that they turned the wolf's stomach so that it was nearly faint with revulsion. "Take your filthy tail," said the wolf, "and get to hell out of my sight, you hound. I can't bear to look at your ugly face."

More dead than alive, Rabchik ran off, so fast he could hardly feel the earth under his feet, afraid even to look around. Running, away . . . away from the forest. Back to the village.

Arrived back in his village, Rabchik over-shot the yard where he had grown up (though he was drawn to the place where he had been constantly beaten, where he had had his foot broken and his back scalded). He found himself instead in the butchers' market among the butchers' dogs, that is, among his own kind.

"Well, look who's here. Where are you from?" the butchers' dogs say, yawning as they get ready for bed.

"To tell the truth, I'm from right here," says Rabchik. "Don't you recognize me. I'm Rabchik."

"Rabchik. Rabchik . . . the name sounds familiar," say the butchers' dogs, pretending not to know him.

"What sort of mark is that on your back?" asks a small dog named Tsutsik, springing impudently at him.

"Must be a sign to make him easy to recognize—or else it's a beauty mark," jokes Rudek, a shaggy red dog.

Sirkeh, a gray bachelor dog with one eye and one ear missing, says, "If it comes to that, I'm the one to tell

you about marks. What he has is a mark of battle—
against other dogs, whole gangs of them."

"Talk, talk. Everyone talks," says Zhuk, a black
dog without a tail. "Let Rabchik talk. He can tell us
better himself."

Rabchik lies down and starts to tell his story, leaving out not the smallest detail. All the dogs listen, except red Rudek, the jokester who interrupts constantly
with his quips.

"Rudek, are you going to shut up?" asks Zhuk, the
black dog with no tail, and gives a great yawn. "Tell,
tell, Rabchik. We like hearing stories after our meals."

Rabchik tells on and on, reciting his doleful story,
but no one is listening. Tsutsik talks quietly with Sirkeh.
Rudek makes jokes, and Zhuk snores louder than ten
soldiers. From time to time he starts from his sleep to
say, "Tell, tell. We like hearing stories after our meals."

Rabchik is up early the next morning. Keeping his
distance, he watches the butchers wielding their
cleavers. Here, a fore-quarter of beef is being hacked,
its neck dangling and dripping blood; there, a hind-
quarter—a lovely treasure, marbled with fat. Rabchik
looks on, swallowing his saliva. The butchers cut the
meat up. From time to time they throw a piece of skin,
or meat, or a bone to the dogs who leap to catch it.
Rabchik watches the dogs outsmarting each other, making skillful jumps in the right places, never missing a
bone. No sooner does a dog catch its share than it
goes off to one side, full of self-importance, and lies
down to preside over its feast, looking about at the
other dogs as if to say, "You see this bone. *My* bone.
I am eating it."

The others pretend not to notice, though they are thinking, "May you choke on your bone; may the plague take you. Gobbling away all morning, and we have to watch you eat. May the worms eat you."

Another dog sneaks off, a piece of skin in its mouth, looking for a corner in which to eat without being seen —afraid of the evil eye.

Still another stands watching an angry butcher shouting and quarreling with his fellows. Fawning, the dog wags its tail and says, "You see this butcher," (they all look as if they were angry), "I know him. I give you my word—he's a fine man, a precious stone, a diamond, with a character of gold. These butchers have a real sympathy for us. Truly, 'Friends of the Dog.' Watch. In a minute, you'll see a bone with meat still on it come flying—hup!" It leaps into the air to give the other dogs the impression it has really caught something worth-while.

A nearby dog calls out, "That one—he's two things: first, a flattering dog, and then, a liar. May the devil take him."

One dog stands at a chopping-block, and the moment the butcher turns his back, it leaps to the block and licks at the blood. Seeing this, several of the dogs bark, betraying it to the butcher, swearing up and down that the dog has stolen a bit of meat. "As we hope to prosper," they say, "we saw it with our own eyes. May we die on the spot if we are not telling the truth. May we choke on the very first bit of bone that we eat. May we never have anything but sheep's horns and hooves to gnaw on."

"Ugh. It's repulsive . . . enough to turn one's stomach," says an old dog nearby who would have been glad to lick a little at the chopping-block itself.

Rabchik thinks: "How will it all end?" Is he merely going to stand by and watch as the dogs leap and snatch. Better to do some leaping and snatching himself. But even as he is considering the matter, several dogs are at his throat, tearing and biting precisely where he is already in great pain.

Rabchik tucks up his tail, finds his way into a corner, lifts his chin and howls.

"Why are you crying?" asks Zhuk, licking his lips after his meal.

"What's to keep me from crying?" says Rabchik. I'm the unluckiest dog in the world. I thought that here, among my own kind, I'd be able to get something. Believe me, I don't usually crawl but I'm dying of hunger. I'm at my last gasp."

"I believe you," says Zhuk with a sigh. "I know about hunger and I understand your situation, but there's no way I can help you. It's been all worked out: here each butcher has his special dog, and every dog his own butcher."

"Is that really fair?" Rabchik says. "What about justice? What about dogmanity? Is it possible that a dog can perish among dogs, that one can die of hunger among those who have fed?"

"I sigh for you," Zhuk says. "It's as much as I can do." He yawns deliciously and gets ready for his usual after-breakfast nap.

"If that's how it is," says Rabchik, plucking up his courage, "I'll go right to the butchers. It may be I can bark one up for myself."

"Go in good health," Zhuk replies. "Just as long as you keep away from *mine*. If you don't, I'll turn you into a tailless dog—like me. Get it?"

Rabchik went directly to the butchers, bypassing

the other dogs. He jumped into the butchers' faces,
wagged his tail. But a loser drags bad luck. One of the
butchers, a huge, playful fellow with broad shoulders,
threw a cleaver at him. Fortunately, Rabchik was a
good jumper, or he would have been hacked in two.
"You're not a bad dancer," quipped Rudik. "Much
better than our Tsutsik. Tsutsik, come and watch some
real dancing."

Tsutsik runs up and jumps right in Rabchik's face.
Rabchik can stand it no longer. He grabs Tsutsik,
throws him down and bites him in the stomach, venting all his misery on him. Then he takes to his heels
and runs off.

At last, all alone in a field, he lies down in the path
and puts his chin between his paws. He feels so deeply
ashamed he does not care if he ever sees the light of
day again. He does not even mind the biting flies that
now attack him. Let them bite; let them tear. To hell
with it.

"It's the end of the world," thinks Rabchik. "When
a dog among dogs, among his own kind, can't survive
a single day, then the world has been turned topsy-
turvy."

translated by Leonard Wolf

SHOLOM ALEICHEM

On Account of a Hat

A story that concerns the misadventures of a rattle-brained Jewish broker in Russia, who chances to be mistaken for a government official, all on account of a hat. Why, if you put a hat with a visor on the head of a poor Jew, do people start calling him, "Your Excellency"? What makes the real difference when it comes to power and social status after all?

"Did I hear you say absent-minded? Now, in our town, that is, in Kasrilevke, we've really got someone for you —do you hear what I say? His name is Sholem Shachnah, but we call him Sholem Shachnah Rattlebrain, and is he absent-minded? Is this a distracted creature? Lord have mercy on us! The stories they tell about him, about this Sholem Shachnah—bushels and baskets of stories—I tell you, whole crates full of stories and anecdotes! It's too bad you're in such a hurry on account of the Passover, because what I could tell you, Mr. Sholom Aleichem—do you hear what I say?—you could go on writing it down forever. But if you can spare a moment, I'll tell you a story about what happened to Sholem Shachnah on a Passover eve—a story about a hat, a true story, I should live so, even if it does sound like someone made it up."

These were the words of a Kasrilevke merchant, a dealer in stationery, that is to say, snips of paper. He smoothed out his beard, folded it down over his neck, and went on smoking his thin little cigarettes, one after the other.

I must confess that this true story, which he related to me, does indeed sound like a concocted one, and for a long time I couldn't make up my mind whether or not I should pass it on to you. But I thought it over and decided that if a respectable merchant and dignitary of Kasrilevke, who deals in stationery and is surely no *litterateur*—if he vouches for a story, it must be true. What would he be doing with fiction? Here it is in his own words. I had nothing to do with it.

This Sholem Shachnah I'm telling you about, whom we call Sholem Shachnah Rattlebrain, is a real-estate broker—you hear what I say? He's always with landowners, negotiating transactions. Transactions? Well, at least he hangs around the landowners. So what's the point? I'll tell you. Since he hangs around the landed gentry, naturally some of their manner has rubbed off on him, and he always has a mouth full of farms, homesteads, plots, acreage, soil, threshing machines, renovations, woods, timber, and other such terms having to do with estates.

One day God took pity on Sholem Shachnah, and for the first time in his career as a real-estate broker—

are you listening?—he actually worked out a deal. That is to say, the work itself, as you can imagine, was done by others, and when the time came to collect the fee, the big rattler turned out to be not Sholem Schachnah Rattlebrain, but Drobkin, a Jew from Minsk province, a great big fearsome rattler, a real-estate broker from way back—he and his two brothers, also brokers and also big rattlers. So you can take my word for it, there was quite a to-do. A Jew has contrived and connived and has finally, with God's help, managed to cut himself in— so what do they do but come along and cut him out! Where's Justice? Sholem Shachnah wouldn't stand for it—are you listening to me? He set up such a holler and an outcry—"Look what they've done to me!"—that at last they gave in to shut him up, and good riddance it was too.

When he got his few cents, Sholem Shachnah sent the greater part of it home to his wife, so she could pay off some debts, shoo the wolf from the door, fix up new outfits for the children, and make ready for the Passover holidays. And as for himself, he also needed a few things, and besides he had to buy presents for his family, as was the custom.

Meanwhile the time flew by, and before he knew it, it was almost Passover. So Sholem Shachnah—now listen to this—ran to the telegraph office and sent home a wire: *Arriving home Passover without fail.* It's easy to say "arriving" and "without fail" at that. But you just try it! Just try riding out our way on the new train and see how fast you'll arrive. Ah, what a pleasure! Did they do us a favor! I tell you, Mr. Sholem Aleichem, for a taste of Paradise such as this you'd gladly forsake your own grandchildren! You see how it is: until you get to Zlodievka there isn't much you can do about it, so you just lean back and ride. But at Zlodievka the fun begins, because that's where you have to change to get onto the new train, which they did us such a favor by running out to Kasrilevke. But not so fast. First, there's the little matter of several hours' wait, exactly as announced in the schedule—provided, of course, that you don't pull in after the Kasrilevke train has left. And at what time of night may you look forward to this treat? The very middle, thank you, when you're dead tired and disgusted, without a friend in the world except sleep—and there's not one single place in the whole station where you can lay your head, not one. When the wise men of Kasrilevke quote the passage from the Holy Book, *"Tov shem meshemon tov,"* they know what they're doing. I'll translate it for you: "We were better off without the train."

To make a long story short, when our Sholem Shachnah arrived in Zlodievka with his carpetbag he was half dead; he had already spent two nights without sleep. But that was nothing at all to what was facing him—he still had to spend the whole night waiting in the station. What shall he do? Naturally he looked around for a place to sit down. Whoever heard of such a thing? Nowhere. Nothing. No place to sit. The walls of the station were covered with soot, the floor was covered with spit. It was dark, it was terrible. He finally discovered one miserable spot on a bench where he had just room enough to squeeze in, and no more than that, because the bench was occupied by an official of some sort in a uniform full of buttons, who was lying there all stretched out and snoring away to beat the band. Who this Buttons was, whether he was coming or go-

ing, he hadn't the vaguest idea, Sholem Shachnah, that
is. But he could tell that Buttons was no dime-a-dozen
official. This was plain by his cap, a military cap with
a red band and a visor. He could have been an officer
or a police official. Who knows? But surely he had
drawn up to the station with a ringing of bells, had
staggered in, full to the ears with meat and drink, laid
himself out on the bench, as in his father's vineyard,
and worked up a glorious snoring.

It's not such a bad life to be a gentile, and an
official one at that, with buttons, thinks he, Sholem
Shachnah, that is, and he wonders, dare he sit next to
this Buttons, or hadn't he better keep his distance?
Nowadays you never can tell whom you're sitting next
to. If he's no more than a plain inspector, that's still all
right. But what if he turns out to be a district inspector?
Or a provincial commander? Or even higher than that?
And supposing this is even Purishkevitch himself, the
famous anti-Semite, may his name perish? Let someone
else deal with him, and Sholem Shachnah turns cold
at the mere thought of falling into such a fellow's
hands. But then he says to himself—now listen to this.
"Buttons", he says, "who the hell is Buttons? And who
gives a hang for a Purishkevitch? Don't I pay my fare
the same as Purishkevitch? So why should he have all
the comforts of life and I none?" If Buttons is entitled
to a delicious night's sleep, then doesn't he, Sholem
Shachnah, that is, at least have a nap coming? After
all, he's human too, and besides, he's already gone two
nights without a wink. And so he sits down on a corner
of the bench and leans his head back, not, God forbid,
to sleep, but just like that, to snooze. But all of a sudden
he remembers—he's supposed to be home for Passover,

and tomorrow is Passover Eve! What if, God have
mercy, he should fall asleep and miss his train? But
that's why he's got a Jewish head on his shoulders—are
you listening to me or not?—so he figures out the
answer to that one too, Sholem Shachnah, that is, and
goes looking for the porter, a certain Yeremei, he knows
him well, to make a deal with him. Whereas he, Sholem
Shachnah, is already on his third sleepless night and is
afraid, God forbid, that he may miss his train, therefore
let him, Yeremei, that is, in God's name, be sure to
wake him, Sholem Shachnah, because tomorrow night
is a holiday, Passover. "Easter," he says to him in Russian and lays a coin in Yeremei's mitt. "Easter, Yeremei,
do you understand, *goyisher kop?* Our Easter." The
peasant pockets the coin, no doubt about that, and
promises to wake him at the first sign of the train—he
can sleep soundly and put his mind at rest. So Sholem
Shachnah sits down gingerly in his corner of the bench,
pressed up against the wall, with his carpetbag curled
around him so that no one could steal it. Little
by little he sinks back, makes himself comfortable, and
half shuts his eyes—no more than forty winks, you
understand. But before long he's got one foot propped
up on the bench and then the other; he stretches out
and drifts off to sleep. Sleep? I'll say sleep, like God
commanded us: with his head thrown back and his hat
rolling away on the floor, Sholem Shachnah is snoring
like an eight-day wonder. After all, a human being, up
two nights in a row—what would you have him do?

He had a strange dream. He tells this himself, that
is, Sholem Shachnah does. He dreamed that he was
riding home for Passover—are you listening to me?—
but not on the train, in a wagon, driven by a thievish

peasant, Ivan Zlodi we call him. The horses were terribly slow; they barely dragged along. Sholem Shachnah was impatient, and he poked the peasant between the shoulders and cried, "May you only drop dead, Ivan darling! Hurry up, you lout! Passover is coming, our Jewish Easter!" Once he called out to him, twice, three times. The thief paid him no mind. But all of a sudden he whipped his horses to a gallop and they went whirling away, up hill and down, like demons. Sholem Shachnah lost his hat. Another minute of this and he would have lost God knows what. "Whoa, there, Ivan old boy! Where's the fire? Not so fast!" cried Sholem Shachnah. He covered his head with his hands —he was worried, you see, over his lost hat. How can he drive into town bareheaded? But for all the good it did him, he could have been hollering at a post. Ivan the Thief was racing the horses as if forty devils were after him. All of a sudden—tppprrru!—they came to a dead stop, right in the middle of the field—you hear me?—a dead stop. What's the matter? Nothing. "Get up," said Ivan, "time to get up."

Time? What time? Sholem Shachnah is all confused. He wakes up, rubs his eyes, and is all set to step out of the wagon when he realizes he has lost his hat. Is he dreaming or not? And what's he doing here? Sholem Shachnah finally comes to his senses and recognizes the peasant—this isn't Ivan Zlodi at all but Yeremei the porter. So he concludes that he isn't on the high road after all but in the station at Zlodievka, on the way home for Passover, and that if he means to get there he'd better run to the window for a ticket, but fast. Now what? No hat. The carpetbag is right where he left it, but his hat? He pokes around under the

bench, reaching all over, until he comes up with a hat
—not his own, to be sure, but the official's, with the
red band and the visor. But Sholem Shachnah has no
time for details and he rushes off to buy a ticket. The
ticket window is jammed; everybody and his cousins
are crowding in. Sholem Shachnah thinks he won't get
to the window in time, perish the thought, and he starts
pushing forward, carpetbag and all. The people see the
red band and the visor and they make way for him.
"Where to, Your Excellency?" asks the ticket agent.
"What's this Excellency, all of a sudden?" wonders
Sholem Shachnah, and he rather resents it. Some joke,
a gentile poking fun at a Jew. All the same he says,
Sholem Shachnah, that is, "Kasrilevke." "Which class,
Your Excellency?" The ticket agent is looking straight
at the red band and the visor. Sholem Shachnah is
angrier than ever. "I'll give him an Excellency, so he'll
know how to make fun of a poor Jew!" But then he
thinks. "Oh, well, we Jews are in *diaspora*"—do you
hear what I say?—"let it pass." And he asks for a ticket
third class. "Which class?" The agent blinks at him,
very much surprised. This time Sholem Shachnah gets
good and sore and he really tells him off. "Third!" says
he. All right, thinks the agent, third is third.

In short, Sholem Shachnah buys his ticket, takes
up his carpetbag, runs out onto the platform, plunges
into the crowd of Jews and gentiles, no comparison in-
tended, and goes looking for the third-class carriage.
Again the red band and the visor work like a charm;
everyone makes way for the official. Sholem Shachnah
is wondering, "What goes on here?" But he runs along
the platform till he meets a conductor carrying a
lantern. "Is this third class?" asks Sholem Shachnah,

putting one foot on the stairs and shoving his bag into
the door of the compartment. "Yes, Your Excellency,"
says the conductor, but he holds him back. "If you
please, sir, it's packed full, as tight as your fist. You
couldn't squeeze a needle into that crowd." And he
takes Sholem Shachnah's carpetbag—you hear what
I'm saying?—and sings out, "Right this way, Your
Excellency, I'll find you a seat." "What the Devil!" cries
Sholem Shachnah. "Your Excellency and Your Excellency!" But he hasn't much time for the fine points; he's
worried about his carpetbag. He's afraid, you see, that
with all these "Excellencies" he'll be swindled out of his
belongings. So he runs after the conductor with the
lantern, who leads him into a second-class carriage.
This is also packed to the rafters, no room even to yawn
in there. "This way please, Your Excellency!" And again
the conductor grabs the bag and Sholem Shachnah
lights out after him. "Where in blazes is he taking me?"
Sholem Shachnah is racking his brains over this "Excellency" business, but meanwhile he keeps his eye on the
main thing—the carpetbag. They enter the first-class
carriage, the conductor sets down the bag, salutes, and
backs away, bowing. Sholem Shachnah bows right back.
And there he is, alone at last.

Left alone in the carriage, Sholem Shachnah looks
around to get his bearings—you hear what I say? He
has no idea why all these honors have suddenly been
heaped on him—first class, salutes, Your Excellency.
Can it be on account of the real-estate deal he just
closed? That's it! But wait a minute. If his own people,
Jews, that is, honored him for this, it would be under-
standable. But gentiles! The conductor! The ticket
agent! What's it to them? Maybe he's dreaming. Sholem

Shachnah rubs his forehead, and while passing down
the corridor glances into the mirror on the wall. It
nearly knocks him over! He sees not himself but the
official with the red band. That's who it is! "All my bad
dreams on Yeremei's head and on his hands and feet,
that lug! Twenty times I tell him to wake me and I even
give him a tip, and what does he do, that dumb ox—
may he catch cholera in his face—but wake the official
instead! And me he leaves asleep on the bench! Tough
luck, Sholem Shachnah old boy, but this year you'll
spend Passover in Zlodievka, not at home."

Now get a load of this. Sholem Shachnah scoops up
his carpetbag and rushes off once more, right back to
the station where he is sleeping on the bench. He's
going to wake himself up before the locomotive, God
forbid, lets out a blast and blasts his Passover to pieces.
And so it was. No sooner had Sholem Shachnah leaped
out of the carriage with his carpetbag than the locomotive did let go with a blast—do you hear me?—one followed by another, and then, good night!

The paper dealer smiled as he lit a fresh cigarette,
thin as a straw. "And would you like to hear the rest of
the story? The rest isn't so nice. On account of being
such a rattlebrain, our dizzy Sholem Shachnah had a
miserable Passover, spending both *seders* among stran-
gers in the house of a Jew in Zlodievka. But this was
nothing—listen to what happened afterward. First of
all, he has a wife, Sholem Shachnah, that is, and his wife
—how shall I describe her to you? *I* have a wife, *you*
have a wife, we all have wives; we've had a taste of
Paradise; we know what it means to be married. All I
can say about Sholem Shachnah's wife is that she's A-

Number-One. And did she give him a royal welcome!
Did she lay into him! Mind you, she didn't complain
about his spending the holiday away from home, and
she said nothing about the red band and the visor. She
let that stand for the time being; she'd take it up with
him later. The only thing she complained about was—
the telegram! And not so much the telegram—you hear
what I say?—as the one short phrase, *without fail*.
What possessed him to put that into the wire: *Arriving
home Passover without fail*. Was he trying to make the
telegraph company rich? And besides, how dare a
human being say "without fail" in the first place? It
did him no good to answer and explain. She buried him
alive. Oh, well, that's what wives are for. And not that
she was altogether wrong—after all, she had been waiting so anxiously. But this was nothing compared with
what he caught from the town, Kasrilevke, that is. Even
before he returned, the whole town—you hear what I
say?—knew all about Yeremei and the official and the
red band and the visor and the conductor's Your Excellency—the whole show. He himself, Sholem Shachnah,
that is, denied everything and swore up and down that
the Kasrilevke smart-alecks had invented the entire
story for lack of anything better to do. It was all very
simple—the reason he came home late, after the holidays, was that he had made a special trip to inspect a
wooded estate. Woods? Estate? Not a chance—no one
bought *that*! They pointed him out in the streets and
held their sides, laughing. And everybody asked him,
'How does it feel, Reb Sholem Shachnah, to wear a cap
with a red band and a visor?' 'And tell us,' said others,
'what's it like to travel first class?' As for the children,
this was made to order for them—you hear what I say?

Wherever he went they trooped after him, shouting, 'Your Excellency! Your excellent Excellency! Your most excellent Excellency!'

"You think it's so easy to put one over on Kasrilevke?"

translated by Isaac Rosenfeld

I. L. PERETZ

━━━━━━◦≪◦≫◦━━━━━━

The Conjuror

*One of the loveliest Jewish folk legends is that the
prophet Elijah, who is supposed to be especially con-
cerned about the troubles of the poor, will descend to
earth from time to time. Disguised as a simple fellow,
he will help some good or pious people. In this charming little tale, I. L. Peretz reworks this legend as a way
of evoking a moment in the life of the east European
Jews.*

━━━━━━◦≪◦≫◦━━━━━━

Once a conjuror showed up in a small Jewish town in
eastern Poland.

And even though he came just before Passover,
during the anxious and costly days when a Jew has
more worries than hair on his head, the man's arrival
caused a great sensation. What an enigmatic fellow!
In shreds and patches, but with a crumpled top hat. A
Jewish face, with God's image on his nose, but—
cleanshaven. And no identity card, and no one ever
saw him eating—not kosher, not unkosher. What a

mystery! If you asked him, "Where ya from?" he'd say, "Paris." "Where ya going?" "London." "Watcha doin' here?" "Lost my way." He seemed to be traveling on foot. He never went to synagogue, not even on the Sabbath before Passover. And if people started getting pushy and crowded around him, he would melt away as if the earth had gulped him down, and then pop up on the other side of the marketplace.

Meanwhile, he hired an auditorium and began performing his tricks.

And what tricks! In full view of the spectators, he would swallow live coals as though they were noodles, and pull a whole medley of ribbons out of his mouth, red ones, green ones, in all the colors of the rainbow and as long as the Jewish Exile. He reached into a boot, and out came sixteen pairs of turkeys, and what turkeys! As big as bears, and alive—they scurried all over the stage. Next, he lifted one boot and scraped golden ducats off the sole, an entire bowlful of golden ducats! The audience cheered, whereupon he whistled, and the air was filled with loaves of straight and braided *challah* flying around like birds, doing a circle dance or a wedding dance beneath the ceiling; and when he whistled again, everything vanished into thin air as though it had never been! Gone were the ribbons, gone the turkeys—poof!

Now we know that black magic can do a thing or two! The wizards of ancient Egypt very likely performed even greater feats. And so the townsfolk wondered: Why was he so poor? A man scrapes ducats off the sole of his boot and he can't even afford a room at the inn; he merely whistles to bake up more loaves of *challah* than the biggest baker, he pulls turkeys out of

his boot—and yet his face looks as if he had just stepped
out of a coffin, and his eyes are ablaze with hunger.

But let's leave the conjuror and turn to Jonah
and his wife Rebecca. Jonah used to deal in timber. He
bought a forest at a fair price, but when the government declared it a natural preserve, he lost his shirt.
Next, he got a job as manager in a lumberyard; but then
they laid him off. That was months earlier, and he had
been out of work ever since. The winter was so awful
you wouldn't wish it on your worst enemy; now, on top
of everything, Passover. And they had already pawned
everything from the ceiling-lamp to the very last pillow.
So Rebecca said, "Go to the Community Passover Fund
and get some money." But Jonah said he had faith;
God would help; he didn't want any handouts. Rebecca
once again started hunting through every nook and
cranny, and up she came with a worn silver spoon—a
miracle, the spoon had been missing for years. Jonah
went and pawned it and donated the tiny sum to the
Passover Fund. "The poor," he said, "come first." Meanwhile, time went on. Passover was just a few weeks
away. He had faith. "God," he said, "doesn't abandon
you!" So be it. Rebecca held her tongue. A woman has
to obey her husband. But another day wore on, and
then another. Rebecca couldn't sleep a wink; she buried
her face in the hay mattress and wept silently so that
Jonah wouldn't hear. There was not a thing in the house
for Passover. And the days were worse than the nights
—at night you can cry your heart out, but in the daytime you have to put up a front. The neighbors gawked
and gaped and goggled, needling her with glances of
pity. Others asked her, "So when are you going to bake
matzos? How are you doing with beets?" Those closer

to her asked, "What's going on with you, Rebecca? If you need anything, we'll lend it to you," and so on.

But Jonah wouldn't accept gifts from anyone, and Rebecca couldn't act against her husband—so she made up all sorts of excuses, and her face grew redder and redder.

The neighbors, realizing things weren't quite in order, hurried over to the Rabbi to get him to do something. The Rabbi, poor man, heard them out, sighed, pondered, and finally answered that Jonah was learned and God-fearing, and if he had faith, then that was that!

Rebecca didn't even have any holiday candles.

And all at once it was Passover.

Jonah, coming home from the synagogue, saw that all the windows around the marketplace were bright and festive; only *his* window stuck out like a mourner at a wedding, like a blind man among the seeing. But he refused to despair: "God willing, we'll still celebrate Passover!" he thought to himself. Entering his home, he cheerfully said, "Happy holiday," and then, more emphatically, "A happy holiday to you, Rebecca!" And Rebecca's tear-soaked voice answered from a dark corner, "A happy holiday to *you*, my husband!" And her eyes glowed out of the dark corner like two live coals. He went over to her and said, "Rebecca, today's a holiday to commemorate the Exodus, don't you see? We mustn't be mournful! And what's there to be mournful about, anyway? If God doesn't want us to have our own *seder*, we'll simply have to make the best of it and go to someone else's. We'll celebrate in some other home. People will take us in everywhere. . . . Tonight all doors are open. The *Haggadah* says, 'Let anyone who is hungry come in and dine.' Come, get your shawl, and we'll go to the first house we find."

Rebecca, who always did her husband's bidding, fought with all her strength to hold back the sobs that were struggling out of her throat. She wrapped herself up in a tattered shawl and was about to set out—but at that very moment, the door opened, and someone walked in and said, "Happy holiday!"

To which they replied, "The same to you," without seeing who had entered.

And the man who had entered said, "I want to be your *seder* guest."

Jonah answered, "We're not having a *seder*."

The guest replied that he had brought the *seder* along!

"In the dark?" Rebecca let a sob escape.

"God forbid!" answered the holiday guest, "there'll be light." And he waved his hand: Abracadabra! And two pairs of silver candlesticks with burning candles appeared and hovered in the middle of the room. The house became bright. Jonah and Rebecca saw that it was the conjuror, and they were so amazed and frightened they couldn't utter a word. They grabbed each other's hands, their eyes and mouths agape. Meanwhile, the conjuror turned to the table, which was standing neglected in a corner, and said, "Okay, my friend, set yourself, and come over here!"

And no sooner had he spoken than a snow-white tablecloth dropped from the ceiling and covered the table, and the covered table began to move, and slid over to the middle of the room and stopped right beneath the candles, and the silver candlesticks descended and came to rest on the table. "And now," said the conjuror, "all we need is Passover seats—so let there be Passover seats!" And three chairs, from three corners of the room, marched over to the table and stationed them-

selves on three sides. The conjuror ordered them to
grow wider, and so they widened out and turned into
easy-chairs. He called out, "Softer!" and they covered
themselves with red velvet, and, presto, white, snow-
white cushions came down from the ceiling, and, at the
conjuror's command, plopped upon the easy-chairs,
which turned into Passover seats. At his bidding, a Passover plate with the *seder* paraphernalia also emerged
and came to rest on the table, followed by red goblets
with bottles of wine, and matzos, and everything you
need for a proper and merry *seder*, including gilt-edged
Haggadahs.

"Do you have water to wash with?" asked the conjuror. "I can bring water, too!"

It was only now that Jonah and Rebecca recovered
from their astonishment. And Rebecca whispered to
Jonah, "Is it all right? What do you think?" Jonah
didn't know what to say. So she advised him, "Go, husband, and ask the Rabbi." But he replied that he
couldn't leave her alone with the conjuror; he wanted
her to go instead. But she said that the Rabbi wouldn't
believe a mere woman; he'd think she was out of her
mind. So the two of them went to the Rabbi, leaving the
conjuror behind with the *seder*.

The Rabbi said that anything fabricated by sorcery
had no substance, because sorcery is merely an optical
illusion. He told them to go home, and if they could
break the matzos and pour the wine into the goblets
and feel the cushions on the seats, then fine . . . it was
all from God, and they could enjoy it.

That was the Rabbi's verdict. And so, their hearts
pounding, they started back. When they came home,
the conjuror was gone, but the *seder* was just as they

had left it. They could feel the cushions, pour the wine, and break the matzos. . . . And now it dawned on them that their visitor was none other than the Prophet Elijah, and so they had a merry holiday.

translated by Joachim Neugroschel

I. L. PERETZ

————◆⧜◆————

A Musician Dies

Hard though life might be, the Jews have traditionally loved music. In the old country, in almost every Jewish town, there was a little group of musicians: a fiddler, a clarinetist, a drummer. In this story, Peretz shows one of them, on his death-bed, gathering his family together and asking them to mark his passing in the way they know best—by making music.

————◆⧜◆————

A skeleton is in the bed, a skeleton covered with yellow, thin, dry skin. Mikhel, the musician, is dying. Mirrel, his wife, sits near him on a chest, her eyes swollen with crying. Their eight sons, all musicians, are spread around the crowded room. Silence. No one speaks to any of the others. The doctor has given up on Mikhel.

There will be nothing to inherit. The local Burial Society will donate his shroud and the grave. The Society of Pallbearers will add a little brandy. There is nothing more to say; all is clear and definite. Only

Mirrel refuses to concede. After everything seemed settled, she began to create a tumult in the synagogue. She has just come from incantations in the graveyard. Now, she keeps insisting, "He is dying because the children are sinful. They aren't pious. They carouse. That is why God is taking their father. The band of musicians is losing its glory. No wedding will be the way it ought to. No Jew will have a true festivity."

God's compassion is great. One must shout, entreat, do something that will move Him. But they, the children, they have no pity. They do not wear the ritual undergarment. Oh, if only it weren't for their sins! She has an uncle—a *shochet*—in heaven. He must be in the top rank. He would not refuse her. When he was living —may his memory be blessed—he would always pet her. Even now, he probably is well-disposed. No doubt he made an effort; he did everything he could. But the sins, the sins! "They ride to gentile dances. Eat gentile bread and butter. God knows what else they eat there! They don't wear the undergarments." Her uncle is trying. But he won't be able to succeed. "Oh, the sins, the sins!"

The sons do not answer. They stare at the floor— each in a corner.

"There is still time," she whimpers. "Children! Hurry and do penance."

"Mirrel," the invalid cries. "Let be. It's no use. Mirrel, I am done for. Mirrel, I want to die." She begins to flare up, "A nice state of affairs. Die. He wants to die. And me? What of me? No! I will not let you die. You must live. You must. I'll make such a scene the spirit won't be able to leave you." A wound that has not healed has apparently opened in her heart.

"Mirrel, let be!" the invalid pleads. "We cursed each other enough when I was alive. Enough! It's not proper when I'm dying. Oh, Mirrel. I have sinned. You too have sinned. It is enough. Let us be silent. I keep feeling how the coldness of death is creeping up along my body from my toes to my heart. Inch by inch, Mirrel, I am dying. Do not scream. It is better this way."

"Because you want to get rid of me," Mirrel interrupts. "That's what you always wanted," she cries bitterly. "Always! You had dark-skinned Peshke in your heart. Oh, misery! Even now he doesn't repent. Even now, now. . . ."

He smiles a bit sadly. "Not only dark Peshke. There were lots of dark ones, fair ones, and some of them were redheads. But, Mirrel, I never wanted to be rid of you! A woman is a woman. That's how it is with musicians. It's remarkable! It draws like a blister. But a wife is a wife! These are two different things. Remember how when Peshke said something bad about you, I gave her a going over, right there in the middle of the street?

"So—hush. Be quiet! A wife is a wife. Unless there is a divorce. My heart will be aching. Mirrel, believe me. I will be longing for you. You, too, my sons. You too have given me enough trouble. But it doesn't matter. As we musicians say, it has all gone into the fiddle. I know, you liked me, but you didn't really respect me. If I took an extra drop of brandy, you would grumble I was a drunkard. It is not right. It is improper to treat a father in this fashion. Still, I had a father and I didn't treat him any better. Enough of that—I forgive you."

He grew tired.

After a few seconds, "I forgive you," he continued. Then, raising his body slightly, he regarded the others.

"Look at them," he suddenly cried. "Oxen. Their eyes screwed into the ground. Can't even count to two. . . ."

"After all—a father is a loss! Even if a drunkard. Uh?"

The youngest raised his eyes. As he did, his lashes trembled. He began to cry. The other brothers followed. In a minute the tiny room was full of lamentations.

The invalid watched—delighted.

"Well," he said suddenly with a new vigor. "Enough. I'm afraid it will make me feel too sorry. Enough. Obey your father."

"You hard-hearted man! Let them cry," Mirrel shouted. "Their tears may help you."

"Mirrel, be silent. I've already told you. I have played my piece. Enough! Hayim, Berel . . . Yonah. All of you. Listen! Hurry! Take up your instruments."

All stared. "I order. I beg you. Please me," said the invalid. "Take your instruments and come close to the bed."

The sons obeyed; they surrounded the bed. Three fiddles, a clarinet, a bass-horn, a trumpet. . . .

"Let me hear," the sick man said, "how the band will play without me.

"Mirrel, please. Ask the neighbor to come in."

The neighbor was the sexton of the Pallbearers Society. At first Mirrel didn't want to go, but her husband looked at her so pleadingly that she had to obey. Afterwards, she used to say that the word "Mirrel" and the look he gave her just before his death were the same as those right after they got married. She would say, "Do you remember, children? his tender voice and eyes?"

The sexton came in. His eyes looked up and down. "Forgive me, Mirrel," he said. "Call in a *minyan*."

"Don't need 'em," said the invalid. "Why would I need a *minyan*? I have my own, my band of musicians. Mirrel, don't go. I don't need a *minyan*."

Turning his body to them, "Listen, children," he said. "Play without me as you played when I was here. Always play right. Never clown at a poor man's wedding. Be respectful to your mother. And now, play my act of confession. The neighbor will recite the words."

And the little house became full of music.

translated by Nathan Halper

ABRAHAM REISEN

———◦◦∞◦◦———

Iron

This is a romantic story, but with a bittersweet twist. The boy is shy, the girl not very encouraging. Between them grows up a mountain of iron, all the clutter of needless stuff that the boy buys from the girl in the hope of reaching her. But. . . .

———◦◦∞◦◦———

A small friendly group of five men between the ages of thirty and thirty-five was engaged in conversation concerning mysticism, spiritualism, and similar obscure themes when they finally reached the topic of language. One of the group, a tall, slim, dark-complexioned man with black curls scattered in charming disarray on his forehead and ardent yet unsatisfied eyes, became excited by this theme. Impatiently he listened to the opinions of the others and begged permission to relate a short episode from his recent past.

"Don't expect anything of supreme interest," he began in a somewhat trembling, embarrassed voice. "What I am going to relate concerns a brief insignificant period in my life which would have long since vanished from my memory if not for a particular word which lies there so firmly embedded that whenever I hear it spoken by someone, or when I myself happen to think of it, I become curiously sad and aware that it has a symbolic meaning for me. That word is *iron*."

"*Iron?*" cried out the others, as with one voice. And one of the group added, "*Iron!* How interesting. Come, tell us."

"*Iron*," the dark-complexioned man whispered, as though revealing a secret. "When you say *copper*, it means nothing to me. *Brass*—a hollow ring. *Tin, pewter, lead*—nothing. But when I hear *iron*, instantly I become so regretful, so melancholy. But why indulge in sentimentality? Let me tell you. Only one thing I beg of you, don't expect the unusual. It's an absurd story—but here's how it goes. . . ."

It was about five years ago. I was then twenty-five and had already been in love twice, both times foolishly disappointed. Nevertheless, I was eager to fall in love again—again to be disappointed, probably. So I went searching for love in the broad streets of the great city, although I knew well that love is not to be found precisely where one searches for it. My first two loves had happened by chance and had vanished the same way. But the longing heart does not calculate; it searches.

One evening I wandered into a wide, noisy Jewish street, one that was full of shops. Mostly girls stood at the open doors. And such pretty girls! I stared into the eyes of each of them although I knew well that this was improper behavior. But there again—a heart! What does a heart know of modesty? I looked deeply into the eyes of these young, demure Jewish daughters and all of them pleased me. Not a single one displeased me.

At last my glance fell on two eyes, two enormous black but cold eyes of a girl standing at the entrance of a store. Immediately I turned towards her. The girl walked into the store, stepped behind the counter, looked at me, and calmly and coldly inquired, "What do you wish?"

Confused, I threw perplexed glances about the store. Wherever my gaze fell, I beheld iron. *Iron!* My God, a store full of iron! I positively did not need any iron. So what was I doing here, in such a store?

"Well, what do you want?" the girl asked again, calmly but more firmly this time.

"Iron!" I called out.

"Iron?" She smiled frigidly, and her dark eyes glinted as iron does. "Very well, this is a store of iron goods. But what exactly do you need?"

Once more I threw wild glances about me. At last my eyes fell on a hammer, a massive hammer somewhat rusted at the edges. Delighted, I called out, "A hammer!"

Upon hearing these words she became gentler. "Yes, I see, a hammer. . . ." All smiles, she handed it to me.

"What beautiful eyes you have! Unusually beau. . . ."

"But it is iron you are buying," she reminded me sternly.

"Yes, of course—iron, iron," I agreed, staring into those large black orbs. "What is the price of this hammer?"

"It's not expensive." Again she had become gentle. "It costs only thirty kopecks."

"Really *cheap!*" I cried enthusiastically, "*very* cheap!"

"In that case, give me the money and take it." Again she became stern. Each of her words rang out dully, like iron rubbing against iron.

I took out a bill and asked for change, all the while staring into her eyes. "Oh, my God, where on earth did you get such eyes?" I inquired while she counted out the change.

"Perhaps you need more iron? My eyes are none of your business," she replied dryly, handing me my change. "Would you like me to wrap it up for you?"

"Yes, of course, wrap it, wrap it up!"

Calmly and coldly she wrapped up the hammer, tied it with a black string, handed it to me, and walked to the door.

I left the store feeling that I had committed the greatest folly. I held the hammer under my arm where it served to cool my blood. Still, I was dreadfully warm. My temples throbbed; I saw spots before my eyes, and that hammer was so heavy, so intolerably heavy. . . .

When I entered my small solitary room it was already eleven o'clock. I unwrapped the hammer, placed it on the table, and contemplated it. On another small table a picture was lying, an old picture. Once it had been nailed to the wall, but for a long time now it had been just lying around. I reproached myself for my incompetence. How I managed to spoil everything! After all, the picture was so exquisite. . . .

Yes, the picture must go on the wall! But where on earth could one get four nails? At this moment I needed nails so badly. Ah, if it weren't so late, I'd run over to my girl of iron. Well, first thing in the morning I would go to the store.

The next day, however, I was in no hurry. I felt timid, even fearful. Those eyes! My God, how those eyes would examine me. . . .

When darkness fell I became more courageous and walked past the store. She was not at the door. I peered inside and saw her standing behind the counter. Having become aware of my glances, she eyed me indifferently, waiting for my approach. I walked in.

"What would you like?"

"Nails."

"We have plenty of those. A lot of nails?"

"No. Just enough to fasten a picture to my wall. It's such a superb picture—if only you could see it!"

She stared at me sternly and repeated her question, "A lot of nails?"

"A dozen. But perhaps you have delicate golden ones?"

"No, only ordinary iron nails."

She poured out black, sharply-pointed nails from a few boxes. They lay scattered on the counter before me, cold and hard. I searched among them, comparing sizes, and finally selected twelve.

"Three cents!" she announced and yawned.

I was offended. "Oh, you're yawning. You're not interested in selling?"

"Do you need anything else?"

"No," I said abruptly, gathering up the nails and wrapping them myself in a piece of paper. I threw a glance at her, then around the store and, unable to leave, I asked, "Besides iron you have nothing else?"

"Only iron."

I left. At home I took the picture and attached it
to the wall with four nails. The remaining eight lay
scattered on the table like orphans.

Well, I comforted myself, I definitely had needed
the hammer and nails. The picture was really beautiful
and it was now hanging directly opposite my bed.
Before falling asleep, I would be able to lie and look
at it. . . . What a magnificent picture!

But what of tomorrow? Besides iron there was
nothing in that store. I surveyed my door—no lock on
it! My landlady had assured me that theft was out of
the question, but who could believe that? There were
such quantities of invaluable papers in my room, and
my suit—wasn't that worth something too? Starting
from now on, the room must be locked. O my God, how
was it possible that I had let it stay like that for so long
without a lock?

The next day I scarcely survived until darkness.
(Extraordinary, but in daylight I lacked the courage to
enter that store.) The girl was standing inside as though
completely cast of iron. Only the two black eyes moved,
looking at me shrewdly and placidly.

"What do you wish?"

"I need a lock."

"Yes, we sell those."

"Please, I beg of you," I cried out, almost in tears,
"you have such unusually beautiful eyes! And what
if I don't need a lock. . . ?"

She stared at me icily and asked, "A big lock or a
small one?"

"Big, a very big one. My room is located in a dangerous street. You understand, I must have a good lock."

She handed me a large heavy lock. I brought it home and, enchanted, called out, "Precisely the lock I need!"

Abruptly he ceased speaking, looked at the others and added, growing somewhat pale:

"I won't keep you any longer—my story may sound like nonsense to you, to me too perhaps—but in the course of one month my room was transformed into an iron shop. All kinds of ironware could be found there: scissors, knives, pliers, locks, keys, and, towards the end, for no good reason, just lengths of iron. All this I had accumulated by purchasing each day another object made of iron. At that time it seemed to me that the whole world was hard and cold and dry like iron. And to this day I am greatly interested in iron."

He remained silent. In the room there was a strange quiet.

translated by Etta Blum

I. D. BERKOWITZ

——⋯⋯⋯——

The Last of the Line

Pride in learning—this was a major force in the life of
the Jews. No one gained as much respect as the man
who knew the word of God and the commentaries of
the rabbis. Here is a story which evokes the tradition of
rabbinical learning as it is maintained by a young man
who seems like a blessing from heaven.

——⋯⋯⋯——

For unbroken generations they served as rabbis in the
village of Muravanka, hidden in an obscure Lithuanian
forest. Their fame reached wherever a Jewish word was
heard, to every synagogue where the music of the Torah
resounded.

The Muravanka rabbis were a solace when hope
was lost, a source of faith when doubt assailed. They
were esteemed and treasured; looked up to, as a child
would to a father who one day would pass on to him a
rare old-fashioned candelabrum to keep fresh his youth-
ful memories.

In dark moments the Muravanka rabbis glowed
like the seven candlesticks of a silver *menorah*.

Long ago Muravanka was even more remote than
today. Engulfed by timber, its ancient houses were
surrounded by gardens of beet and onion. Hops on
dense vines laced the wooden fences. Prosperous Jews
dressed in linen coats strolled about, venting clouds of
smoke from pipes tamped tight with dried cabbage
leaves. Resin tapped in the forest supported the village,
and a Jewish home never lacked corn bread and barley
soup. A new mouth to feed caused no concern. The
Lord was blessed. The bucket lowered into the well,
water added to the pot simmering with barley—and the
infant introduced to his staple diet.

If a daughter blossomed and her father was unable
to provide a bride's needs, he took down his walking
stick, dressed in his white shirt with the broad rolled-
down collar, said the prayer for a safe journey, and set
out for Vohlin, that wonder city, where in the middle
of the week white bread was served with saffron, and
occasionally even with honey.

There in Vohlin, one Friday before sundown, a
wealthy Jewish shopkeeper—staid, heavy-set, with a
thick yellow beard—paced in his study. His hips too
wide for his plaited silk belt, at peace with himself, he
sang out, "Gree-etings!," accenting the vowels and
snapping his plump fingers for emphasis. His guest for
the Sabbath—a poor elderly scholar—sat in a corner, his
eyes fixed on the floor. Perhaps he was awed by the
richly furnished study, or perhaps he thought of home,
where his wife waited with his daughter, who was suddenly mature enough to be a bride. He missed his
isolated village with its hard-working Jews, tapping
resin all week, then gathering in the sweltering synagogue, where their celebrated scholars swayed with

candles in their hands over the massive volumes of the
Talmud.

At the table, overwhelmed by the odors of *gefilte
fish* and *knishes* soaking in fat, the scholar could not
restrain himself and blurted out:

"But in Muravanka we have a rabbi!! Well—"

The scholar spoke with a touch of conceit. His
piercing dark eyes caught the fire of his emotion. He
recalled Muravanka's famed sages, their keen minds,
unlimited patience—studying day and night—sleeping
a half hour in every twenty-four beside the heavy, open
Torahs, their heads, like those of weary lions, dropping
in the light of candles which flickered on silent guard.
Each dawn the congregation came into the synagogue
cautiously, fearful lest it disturb the scholars in their
murky corner.

"That's how we study Torah in Lithuania!"

The burly shopkeeper listened attentively, loosen-
ing the silk belt on his Sabbath gaberdine and un-
buttoning the jacket pressing his bloated stomach.
Puffing out his cheeks, the shopkeeper shook his head,
"Why should anyone doubt a Lithuanian?"

Some time later the wealthy shopkeeper passed
through the provinces. Curiosity drove him to see for
himself the rabbi of Muravanka. The sight of the rabbi
evoked fear and wonder, reminding him of the first time
he stood at the foot of a mountain, straining to make
out its peak. The rabbi's tufted eyebrows and knowing
eyes, his stern forehead chiseled as deeply as marble,
terrified the shopkeeper. The rabbi spoke coldly, with
intensity and a doggedness that would not yield easily
to mercy. From the chiseled forehead and shaggy eyebrows tumbled the force of the Divine Manifestation.

Such were the renowned rabbis of Muravanka.

A single family gave Muravanka its unbroken line of rabbis. They were tall, heavy-boned Jews with dense, curly beards which rarely showed a trace of gray, even in old age. Disciplined and restrained, they heard and saw much, but spoke as a rule by lifting their thickset eyebrows or creasing a deeply furrowed forehead. It was considered unusual to hear a Muravanka rabbi say as much as:

"Well—"

The rabbinate passed from father to son, and as well as his position, the son inherited a salary of eighteen guilden a week, a lectern scorched by millennia of candles burned down to the wick, a heavy, pitted walking stick, and a silk caftan, burnished with wear, whose shine dazzled the eyes under a summer Sabbath sun.

Years and years ago, when the Jews first came, Muravanka was inhabited by fierce dogs and thieves sporting monstrous mustaches. Soon after the Jews settled, a tall young man appeared in the synagogue at dawn on the seventh day of *Succoth,* apparently from a distant village. His feet were bare, his trousers rolled up and his shoes dangling beside a fresh truss of willow twigs from the pitted walking stick on his shoulder. The children seized the willow twigs to thump on the desk during the *Succoth* prayer. Clustering around the stranger, the congregation showered him with questions: "Who are you? Where is your home? Are your mother and father alive? Why are you here? Are you married?" The young man, lowering his eyes, was silent. At last he spoke four words:

"I wish to learn."

The young man remained in the study house. In Muravanka the villagers began to speak with reverence about his quality of stubbornness—and how the tall

barefoot young man, appearing from neither here nor
there, was succeeding in his determination to become
a scholar. Winter nights he opened the stove to study
in the glimmer of embers. Once for three days and
nights he forgot to eat or drink as he stood pondering
an intricacy of the Talmud, his forehead wrinkled and
his eyes glowing, the pitted walking stick held rigidly
in his hand, not a muscle stirring. When the answer
came to him he shouted, "Well!" and rapped the stick
against the lectern, startling the congregation as it was
softly reciting the eighteen blessings.

The young man became the rabbi of Muravanka,
and passed on his vitality to his sons and his sons' sons.
They succeeded each other, these titans, each generation increasing in vigor, all stubborn in their faith, their
eyebrows dark and tangled, their foreheads furrowed,
their eyes stern and piercing.

Muravanka basked in the light of seven suns. The
study house teemed with scholars, voices young and
old blending in prayer and song over the Talmud.
Fathers and uncles, grimy and weary from tapping resin
all week in the forest, would drift in between the afternoon and evening prayers, cluster around the stoves, and
listen. Jewish drivers, ferrying passengers through the
forest, would slip into the synagogue early in the morning, riding crops tucked under their armpits, to overhear
a commentary on the Talmud. Outside, housewives
washing at the well beat the wet laundry in cadence to
the melody of the Torah, which wafted into the street
like sweet tidings.

The fame of Muravanka spread. From year to year
the distinction of its rabbis grew, and among Jews
there was a belief that if the line survived to the tenth

generation, Jewry would receive, if it pleased God, a special grace.

But the line did not survive to the tenth generation. The ninth was the last.

Neither of the two sons of the ninth rabbi of Muravanka brought him comfort. They brooded a great deal, asked odd questions, and eventually left the village.

Once a rumor reached Muravanka that the elder son had published a book in one of the great cities and now was called "professor." At first the rabbi lowered his eyes and said nothing. Then he looked up and observed:

"Well—"

Not another word. Thereafter the rabbi's color seemed to fade, and his expression grew more knowing and more firm.

Nothing further was heard about his sons and they were not discussed in the rabbi's presence, since he himself never mentioned them.

Then one Sabbath before Passover something unexpected happened in the house of study. The rabbi was standing at the Holy Ark wrapped in his prayer shawl. The ancient synagogue was full. The rabbi's voice, clear and resonant, cast a spell over the congregation.

Without warning the rabbi broke off. The congregation shuddered and waited. For a moment the rabbi gazed at his audience. Turning, he parted the curtain over the Ark, opened its doors slowly, and said:

"Jews, listen! I know what many of you are think-

ing. You're asking yourselves as I am: what right have
I to teach the Torah when my own sons have forsaken
it? Standing before the Holy Scroll I say to you: I have
no sons! Of our line of teachers, I am the last. . . ."

Years passed, but the rabbi's bearing remained
erect and his dense beard did not gray. Late at night,
just before dawn, he still would appear on the street—
a tall, spare elderly man—his walking stick in one hand
and a lantern in the other, hurrying to study alone in
the ancient synagogue.

And then Muravanka began to buzz about its new
prodigy.

He was the son of a poor tailor. Thin, pale, with a
steep nose and quick eyes, he had left the village after
his *Bar Mitzvah*. Soon word drifted back that he was
developing into a luminary who would outstrip the
keenest minds of the era. He had a rare quality: he was
able to reduce to dust massive roadblocks to the understanding of the Talmud. Numerous centers of learning
sent emissaries to induce him to become their rabbi.

At the same time Muravanka was becoming uneasy
because its rabbi was old—his days numbered—and he
had no successor.

The village turned to the rabbi and asked his advice. Should they consider inviting the prodigy, the
tailor's son, to take the rabbi's place after he was gone,
in a hundred and twenty years? No one else seemed
worthy of following the Muravanka sages.

The old rabbi listened and lowered his thickset
brows. Without lifting his eyes he answered with one
word:

"Well—"

Muravanka dispatched a spokesman to the prodigy, offering him the rabbinate, and before long the news spread: he's coming!

The villagers prepared to meet the young man on the outskirts of town. The old rabbi asked to be taken along, and a bench was prepared for him.

The meeting took place on a Friday in the forest where Jews tapped resin all week for a livelihood. Out of the lingering autumn light a wagon appeared, churning dust. The celebrated young scholar was driven up and the villagers surged about, extending their welcomes. His father, the elderly tailor, braced himself against a tree and in a loud voice cried with joy.

At this point the rabbi decreed that the prodigy would not be permitted to enter Muravanka before the rabbi had heard him expound the Torah.

The prodigy accepted this condition. The Jews, including women and children, formed a circle, all eyes fixed expectantly on the tailor's son.

Standing in the wagon, the young man began to speak. At first he seemed muddled. Hesitantly, his gaze fluttered over the heads of his listeners. Soon, however, his features were ignited by a trend of thought. Words came rapidly. Not customary words from the customary Torah as commonly understood, but flashing perceptions. One after the other. Each one blazing forth before its forerunner dimmed.

The old rabbi sat on the bench, leaning against his pitted walking stick. As he listened, bitter thoughts assailed him. The thin young man with the steep nose and quick eyes, his fingers darting in the air for stress, was no more than a tailor himself, stitching words.

"Yes, you sew better than your father—" the rabbi

felt like saying. But he remained silent, his brow ruf-
fled and unmoving, his eyes lowered. When the prodigy
had finished, the villagers turned to the rabbi, who
continued to sit still as a post. Many wondered whether
in his old age he had fallen asleep.

Suddenly the bush was broken by the sound of
splintering. On his bench, the rabbi quivered and
lurched. The villagers who rushed to his side found his
walking stick shattered.

Faint, his shoulders bent, the rabbi arose and faced
his anxious congregation. He extended his hand slowly
in the direction of the village and said quietly to the
prodigy:

"Well. Now you may enter. . . ."

That Friday evening the rabbi came to the synagogue like a mourner, without his silk caftan. The congregation watched as he led the prodigy to the Holy
Ark, seated him beside the lectern and said:

"You will sit here."

The rabbi left the platform and took his place
among the poor guests visiting the synagogue.

For a moment the congregation sat stunned, then
broke into a lamentation. Young and old wept openly.
The prodigy sat beside the lectern, shivering like a child
seized by fever.

The old rabbi stood and straightened his stooped
shoulders and ordered:

"No tears."

It happened before the High Holidays. To this day
the villagers remember those weeks. The skies were
red, as if licked by flame. Jews stood about wearily,
thoughtful. Infants nestled against their mothers' aprons.

On Yom Kippur, as the last prayer approached, word spread that the old rabbi, dressed in his prayer shawl and solemn white linen robe, had passed away.

The prodigy survived him only briefly. He died in his father's cottage, and was buried on the seventh day of *Succoth* under a biting autumn rain. The villagers were certain that he had been summoned by the Muravanka rabbi for a hearing before the divine rabbinical court.

translated by Reuben Bercovitch

ISAAC METZKER

———•⧓•———

White Feet

Most Jews in eastern Europe lived in small towns. Still, a few did manage to earn a living of sorts as farmers, and their life seems to have been a little better and healthier. In this story, we get a glimpse of a Jewish family in the country, vital and close-knit. A girl comes to visit from the city. Wittingly or not, she creates a rivalry between the two country brothers who have, until then, been as close as twins.

———•⧓•———

With faces fiery from the hot sun and their trousers rolled to their knees, the two brothers stood in the swampy valley and cut the green rushes with their sickles. They tied the plants in large bundles and carried them home on their shoulders to decorate the house and yard for *Shevuoth*. When they were going home with the last two bundles, they stopped near the river to wash their feet for the holiday.

Like two friends who always have something to tell each other, they sat down near the water, one beside the other. They were in no hurry to go home. The

sun had dried off their reddish-brown overgrown feet
and spread a glistening over them. Between the sun
and the valley lay the remainder of the day. Little by
little the brightness moved across the valley with its
yellow buttercups and spread out over the colorful
meadows. They both looked into the water, where their
broad faces were reflected. Sleepy beetles, who had
fallen from the trees during the day like dry fruit, were
swimming about. The brothers told each other about
the last night, when they had not been together. One
of them had spent the whole night in the mill sifting
flour for the holiday, while the other had gone fishing
with some friends and had brought home several large
carp.

"Look, our clover has grown little heads," one suddenly burst out delightedly.

"Like a full-blown brush," the other exclaimed.
Their arms around each other's shoulders, they gazed
with quiet pleasure over the field of clover in the distance, which had just caught the glow from the sun.

The younger was the first to turn his eyes away
from the clover field, and for a long time he stared at the
five thick toes on each of their newly-washed feet. They
had exactly the same bent girth and the same twisted
toenails.

"Our toes look like barrels. They're getting wider
and wider." He turned his face to his brother and saw
how the other was holding his upper lip stretched out.

"Our mustaches are already beginning to sprout."
The elder smiled and ran his finger along his upper lip.

"Yours will start growing sooner. You're eleven
months older than I," said the younger, looking down
at his lip.

"You know, you can't see when blond hair begins to grow."

"Yes, that's true, you can't see when it begins to grow."

"And Papa said he was twenty years old before his mustache began to grow."

"First he grew a beard and then a mustache."

Each looked at the thin white fuzz on the other's ruddy face and talked about their old papa, Israel. He hadn't grown a beard or a mustache, and without his long earlocks, his round clean-shaven face would have looked like a priest's.

"We have to get the food ready for the horse and cows for the holiday."

"And we haven't cleaned the stable yet," both suddenly realized. They divided the bundles and started for home.

Along the way, every time one tossed out a few words, the other would either keep consenting or repeating what was said.

"In the morning, after we pray and eat, we'll take the horse into the woods."

"He can pasture where it's cool."

"Papa has probably come home from the city already."

"Yes, he's probably home already."

In front of the gate they both suddenly stopped and stared in wonderment at the decorated hearth and at their scrubbed house with its whitewashed walls. A young girl was sitting in front of the door of the house, and she had taken off her shoes and socks. Both brothers looked at her feet, which were as white and delicate as though they had been carved out of new wood.

"Look at her feet."

"White as snow," both exclaimed simultaneously.

The girl soon noticed them, got up from the ground, and remained standing like a slender birch tree. Eyes cast down, the two boys began to move along the fence, looking stealthily every once in a while at her white feet.

"It's Rivka, Aunt Chaya's daughter. She came all alone by train—an unexpected guest for *Shevuoth.*" Their mother appeared at the door of the house. Their mother's remarks made the two brothers feel more comfortable and they came closer.

"Which one is my age?" asked Rivka, and just like a city girl, in fact, like a grownup, she held out her right hand, first to the younger and then to the elder.

"They're twins," their proud mother joked, her hands on her cheeks.

"I'm—at Passover I'll be fourteen."

"And I'm eleven months older than both of you." Soon, one after the other, the brothers burst out talking and their faces and ears became red as beets.

After this conversation they stood there with half-open mouths, not knowing what to do with their hands. They looked at each other, eyes blinking, and again stole sideways glances at Rivka's white feet. Then they went away to prepare food for the horse and cows.

"When papa hits one, the other cries," their mother told Rivka, gazing with maternal pleasure after her two sons.

"How grownup she is already. And her feet are— the miller's wife Baba doesn't have such feet—" the elder mused on his way to the stable, as though talking to himself.

"Rivka never goes barefoot," the younger wanted to insist, but different words came out of his mouth.

"She's the same age as me," burst out of him in a voice not his own. In silence, both rushed through their chores. They quickly cut a whole mountain of hay, threw the sheafs into the stalls, stirred the tubs, and not a word passed between them.

In the evening the whole household sat outside by the front door. The air was full of the scent of blooming lilac and the buzzing of the wide-awake beetles and bugs. The evening was serene, the sky chockful of stars. Rivka, dressed entirely in white, sat between them and chattered on and on. She told about her father and mother, about the city, and she told how on her way from the station in town she got lost on another road. Then a farmer had shown her the way and told her to turn right near the white cross.

During the whole evening both boys longed to interrupt Rivka's conversation. They each had something to say, but a heaviness settled in their heads and around their hearts and seized hold of their tongues. They sat, staring at Rivka's pretty white face and listening to her chatter until their mother sent everyone to bed.

The brothers were accustomed to going to bed face to face, talking to each other until they fell asleep. But now they lay turned away from one another, back to back, and were silent. They turned and twisted on their bed and their eyes would not close.

Late at night the elder got up and bent over the younger's face.

"Why aren't you sleeping?" he asked angrily.

"And why aren't you sleeping?" asked the younger, even more angrily.

Until dawn they kept staring at the ceiling and the shadowy walls.

The next day they didn't lead the horse into the woods; they both hung around Rivka. Little by little they got closer to her and each tried to outdo the other in conversation and friendliness. When one showed her how to get honey out of the little flower-cups, the other caught a bee, ripped it in half, and drew a whole little sack of honey out of it. When the younger showed Rivka a pair of young doves down from the attic, the elder deftly scrambled up to the top of an old peartree and from on high showed her a nest of naked baby birds. Climbing down from the tree, the elder slipped on a broken branch and bloodied his foot. When the younger saw him hanging in the air with his bloody foot, a singular joy suddenly overcame him and he let out such a hearty laugh that Rivka looked at him with large questioning eyes.

For the two days of *Shevuoth* both brothers kept following Rivka around, reluctant to leave her for a minute. When their mother called them to go on an errand, they didn't run to her, one after the other, as usual, but instead haggled with each other.

"Go on, mama's calling."

"No, you go."

"I already brought water once today, you go."

Meanwhile Rivka was happily jumping about on her sparkling white feet, laughing out loud and dancing first towards one and then the other.

By the second evening of *Shevuoth*, Rivka was ready to go home. A neighbor, who was supposed to leave for the train at the first star, had promised to take her. Meanwhile, until the sun had set completely, both brothers were turning a rope in the middle of the yard while Rivka jumped over it.

"Ten, twenty, thirty, forty—" she counted, jumping

and gloomily watching the sun, which was setting little by little.

"Bring in some wood." They heard a voice from the house. The boys looked at each other like two cocks before they start to fight, and neither stopped turning the rope.

"There's not a stick of wood in the house," their mother shouted to them.

"Can't you hear?"

"Can't *you?*"

Fiercely, eyes blazing, they continued to turn the rope, until Rivka stopped jumping.

"Go, both of you," Rivka shouted at them.

They both went to the woodshed, and Rivka went into the house.

The younger seized a few sticks from the woodpile and started out of the shed.

"Look how he takes it with one finger." And the elder boiled over with wild rage.

The younger had never heard such a strange angry voice from the elder. He stared at him as he went out. His brother's rage so chilled his heart that he felt anxious to get back to the house quickly. He heard the angry voice as though it were not meant for him, calling to him to take more wood.

In a murderous fury the elder threw down the wood he was holding, seized an axe whose blade sparkled from a corner, and made for his younger brother. The blade did not strike him, but the handle fell across his path. It made the younger brother's head feel dizzy. The few white pieces of wood in his hand danced before his eyes like Rivka's white feet, and he fell full length on the ground.

In an instant, the younger was on his feet again, and with the axe in his hand, he lunged furiously after his brother. Meanwhile, Rivka came out of the house with her suitcase in her hand and went up to them. She reached out her hand like a grownup, first to one, and then the other, and said goodbye.

Both brothers followed her to the door and watched her going down the road. When they could no longer see the wagon that was taking Rivka to the train, they sat down together on the doorstoop.

The two boys were silent. Dark night had blotted out the lilacs, the white blossoms on the trees, and the gleaming blade of the axe, which lay in the middle of the yard. Both were silent, as with warm glistening eyes, they gazed out into the dark night.

translated by Ruth Whitman

ISAAC BASHEVIS SINGER

———— ⋅◆⋅ ————

The Oath

Of all living Yiddish writers, Isaac Bashevis Singer has gained the greatest reputation among American readers in recent years. One of his most popular books is In My Father's Court, *a series of sketches that turn back to his childhood and youth, and deal with Jewish life in Poland a half century ago. They give a brilliant picture of that life, especially, as in* The Oath, *of the moral strength which Jews could derive from their deep religious convictions.*

———— ⋅◆⋅ ————

Whenever he conducted a *Din Torah*, or rabbinical trial, Father repeated the same speech: that he was opposed to the taking of oaths. Not only did he object to oaths, he objected even to pledges, words of honor, or handshaking as guarantees for the fulfillment of a promise. One can never fully trust one's own memory, Father argued; therefore, one must not swear even to what one believes to be the truth. It is written that when God proclaimed, "Thou shalt not take the name of the Lord . . . ," heaven and earth trembled.

I would often picture this scene in my imagination: Mount Sinai enveloped in flames; Moses standing there, holding the Tablets of the Law. Suddenly an awesome voice is heard—the voice of God. The earth begins to totter and quake, and with it all the mountains, the seas, the cities, and the oceans. The heavens tremble, together with the sun, the moon, the stars. . . .

But the woman with the large black matron's wig, with the masculine face and the Turkish shawl draped around her shoulders, absolutely craved to take an oath. I no longer remember what that *Din Torah* was about. I remember only that it involved the one woman and several men. They accused her of something. Perhaps it was in connection with a legacy, or about monies that had been concealed. It did involve, if I recall correctly, a rather large sum. The men spoke harsh words; they pointed their fingers accusingly at the woman. They called her a swindler, a thief, and all sorts of insulting epithets. But the woman did not take it without protest. She had an answer for every argument. For every insult, she hurled back an insult or a curse. Hair sprouted on her upper lip—a woman's mustache. On her chin there was a wen from which grew a small, pointy beard. Her voice was rough like a man's, full of vigor. Yet, although she was an aggressive woman, apparently she could not swallow the accusations. After each one she would shriek: "Rabbi, light the black candles and open the Ark! I want to swear by the Purity [the Torah scroll]!"

Father was shaken. "Hasten not to swear oaths!"

"Rabbi, it is permissible to swear to the truth. I am ready to swear before black candles!"

The woman must have come from the provinces, for the women of Warsaw were not familiar with such

oaths and expressions. She clenched her hand into a
fist and hit Father's table so that the tea glasses
trembled. Every few minutes she ran to the door, as
though she were ready to escape and leave the others
sitting there. But soon she would return with new pro-
testations of her innocence and new arguments against
her accusers. Suddenly she blew her nose so violently
and with such a trumpeting sound that one might have
thought someone had blown a *shofar*. I stood behind
my father's chair, frightened. I was afraid that this
Tartar of a woman would go completely wild—break
the table, the chairs, father's lectern; tear the books;
beat the men mercilessly. Mother, a frail person, opened
the door every few minutes and looked in. An uncanny
force emanated from this woman.

The argument grew more and more heated. One
man, with a reddish nose and a small gray beard, found
his courage anew and began to accuse the woman once
more of being a liar, an embezzler, and such like names.
Suddenly the woman jumped up. I thought she would
pounce upon the little gray man and kill him on the
spot. But she did something quite different. She flung
open the door of the Holy Ark, impetuously took hold of
the Torah scroll inside, and called out in a heart-rending
voice: "I swear by the sacred scroll that I am telling the
truth!"

Then she enumerated all the assertions to which
she was swearing.

Father jumped up as though to tear the scroll out
of her hands, but it was too late. Her adversaries stood
motionless, petrified. The woman's voice became hoarse,
was broken by sobs. She kissed the coverlet of the scroll
and began to cry with such a broken, wailing voice that

one was reminded of an excommunication or a funeral.

For a long time there was a heavy silence in the study. Father stood, his face pale, and shook his head as if in negation. The men stared at each other, confused, perplexed. There was, obviously, no more to be said, nothing further to be argued. The woman left first. Then the men left. Father stood for a while in a corner and wiped the tears from his eyes. All these years he had avoided taking even a pledge—and now a woman had sworn by the Torah, in our house, before our scroll. Father feared a harsh retribution. Mother paced the kitchen, deeply upset. Father walked over to the Ark, opened the door slowly, moved the scroll, straightened the scroll holders. It was almost as though he wanted to ask the scroll's forgiveness for what had happened.

Usually after a *Din Torah*, Father would talk over the arguments with the family, but this time all remained silent. It was almost as though the adults had made a pact not to mention the incident by so much as a word. For days an ominous silence hung over our house. Father lingered over his prayers in the Hasidic study house. He no longer chatted with me. Once, however, he said he had only one request to make of the Almighty: that he might no longer have to earn his living as a rabbi. I frequently heard him sigh his familiar sigh and whisper the plea: "Ah, woe is us, dear Father. . . ." And sometimes he would add: "How much longer? How much longer?"

I knew what he meant: how much longer will this bitter exile last? How much longer will the Evil One hold sway? . . .

Slowly we began to forget the incident. Father again became approachable, began to tell stories and to repeat Hasidic lore. The *Din Torah* had taken place during the summer. Then came the Three Weeks of Mourning for the destruction of the temple, followed by the Nine Days, and the Ninth of Ab. Then on the Fifteenth of Ab, Father again began to study in the evenings. The month of *Elul* came, and in the Hasidic synagogue in our courtyard the *shofar* was sounded every day to frighten away Satan, the accuser. Everything was taking place just as in every other year. Father would rise early. By seven he had already performed the morning ablution and was preparing to study his daily portion of the Talmud. He made his preparations quietly, so as not to wake Mother and the children.

But one morning, at the break of day, we heard a tempestuous knocking on the outer door. Father was alarmed. Mother sat up in bed. I jumped out of my bed. No one had ever knocked on our door so early in the morning. People do not come to ask ritual questions before the day has fully dawned, nor to settle disputes. Knocking with such force and anger for us could mean only the police. On the Sabbath a small congregation gathered in our house for prayers, and for this we had no license. Father always lived in the fear that he might, God forbid, be imprisoned. According to Russian law he was not even licensed to perform weddings or to grant divorces. True, by way of a certain "fixer" he regularly sent small sums to the local precinct chief and captain. But who knows what the Russian police would suddenly decide to do? Father was afraid to open the door. He did not speak a word of Russian or Polish. Mother put on her robe and went to the door. I crept into my pants and boots, and followed her. I was thrilled

at the prospect of seeing a uniformed policeman right
in our house. Mother began to speak Polish even before
she opened the door.

"*Kto tam?*"

"Open the door!" a voice was heard in Yiddish.

I ran to tell Father the good news that the stranger
was a Jew and not a policeman. He quickly praised the
Lord of the Universe.

I rushed back into the kitchen, where, to my
astonishment, I recognized the woman who had sworn
the oath before the Torah scroll. A little later Mother
brought her into the study. Father entered from the
bedroom.

"Hmm, what is it?" he asked irritably.

"Rabbi, I am the woman who swore the oath. . . ."
she began.

"Hmmm, nu? Nu?"

"Rabbi, what I have to tell you is confidential."

"Leave the room," Father said to the family.

Mother went out and took me with her. I had a
tremendous desire to eavesdrop, but the woman had
cast a gloomy look upon me, indicating that she was
wise to my tricks. Her face had become gaunter,
pointier, ashen. From the study I could hear a mum-
bling, sighs, a silence, then again a muttering. Something was happening in there on that cool *Elul* morning,
but I could not discover what it was. Mother went back
to bed. I also undressed again. But although I was tired
and my eyelids were heavy, I could not fall asleep. I
was waiting for Father to return, but an hour passed
and they were still whispering secrets in the study. I
was just beginning to doze off when the door opened
and Father entered. His face was white.

"What happened?" asked my mother.

"Oh, woe, woe!" answered my father. "Woe is us—this is the end of the world, the end of all ends!"

"What is it?"

"It were better not to ask. It is time for the Messiah to come! Everything is in such a state . . . 'for the waters are come in unto my soul. . . .'"

"Tell me what happened!"

"Alas, the woman swore falsely. She has been able to find no rest. She confessed of her own free will. Think of it: she swore falsely before a Torah scroll!"

Mother remained seated on her bed, silent. Father began to sway, but there was in his swaying something different from other days. His body rocked back and forth like a tree tossed by a storm wind. His earlocks quivered with every motion. Outside, the sun was rising and cast a reddish net over his face, and his beard glowed like a flame.

"What did you say to her, Father?"

Father looked angrily toward my bed. "What, you are not asleep? Go back to sleep!"

"Father, I heard everything!"

"What did you hear? The evil inclination is strong, very strong! For a little money, one sells one's soul! She took an oath, an oath before the Torah! . . . But she has repented. Despite everything, she is a true Jewess. Repentance helps in every need!" Father exclaimed suddenly. "Even Nebuzradan, when he repented, was granted forgiveness. There is no sin that cannot be wiped out by penitence!"

"Will she have to fast?"

"First of all, she has to return the money, for it is written: 'That he shall restore which he took violently away. . . .' Soon it will be Yom Kippur. If one repents with all one's heart, the Almighty—blessed be His name —forgives. He is a merciful and forgiving God!"

I heard later that nightmares had tortured the woman. At night she could not sleep. Her dead father and mother appeared to her in her dreams, dressed in shrouds. My father imposed a penitence upon her, to fast Mondays and Thursdays, to give money to charity, to abstain from meat for some time, except on the Sabbath and holidays. In addition she must have returned the money, for I recall seeing, one more time in our house, the men who had accused her.

Years later Father still told this story. If ever, during a *Din Torah*, anyone mentioned an oath, he would tell the story of this woman. To me it always seemed that the Torah scroll, too, remembered, and that whenever Father retold the incident, there, on the other side of the velvet curtain that covered the Ark, the scroll was listening. . . .

from In My Father's Court,
translated by Channah Kleinerman-Goldstein,
Elaine Gottlieb, and Joseph Singer

ISAAC BASHEVIS SINGER

The Purim Gift

When life is hard, people take special pleasure in their holidays. For the Jews in eastern Europe, the holiday of Purim was one in which everyone could relax into playfulness, and children were encouraged to be a little mischievous. Here's a story about an exchange of Purim gifts that led to some unexpected trouble.

Our home was always half unfurnished. Father's study was empty except for books. In the bedroom there were two bedsteads, and that was all. Mother kept no foods stocked in the pantry. She bought exactly what she needed for one day and no more, often because there was no money to pay for more. In our neighbors' homes I had seen carpets, pictures on the walls, copper bowls, lamps, and figurines. But in our house, a rabbi's house, such luxuries were frowned upon. Pictures and statuary were out of the question; my parents regarded them as idolatrous. I remember that in the *heder* I had once bartered my *Pentateuch* for another boy's, because the frontispiece of his was decorated with pictures of Moses holding the Tablets and Aaron wearing the priestly robe and breastplate—as well as two angels. Mother saw it and frowned. She showed it to my father. Father declared that it is was forbidden to have such pictures in a sacred book. He cited the Commandment: "Thou shalt not make unto thee any graven image, or any likeness. . . ."

Into this stronghold of Jewish puritanism, where the body was looked upon as a mere appendage to the soul, the feast of Purim introduced a taste of luxury.

All the neighbors sent Purim gifts. From early afternoon the messengers kept coming. They brought wine, mead, oranges, cakes, and cookies. One generous man sent a tin of sardines; another, smoked salmon; a third, sweet-and-sour fish. They brought apples carefully wrapped in tissue paper, dates, figs—anything you could think of. The table was heaped with delicacies. Then came the masked mummers, with helmets on their heads and cardboard shields and swords, all covered with gold or silver paper. For me it was a glorious day. But my parents were not pleased with this extravagance. Once a wealthy man sent us some English ale. Father looked at the bottle, which bore a colorful label, and sighed. The label showed a red-faced man with a blond mustache, wearing a hat with a feather. His intoxicated eyes were full of a pagan joy. Father said, in an undertone, "How much thought and energy they expend on these worldly vanities."

Later in the day Father would treat the Hasidim with the wine. We did not eat the Warsaw cakes, for we were never certain just how conscientious Warsaw Jews were about the dietary regulations. One could not know whether the pastries had been baked with chicken fat and must therefore not be eaten together with any milk foods.

The mummers, too, were disposed of quickly, for the wearing of masks and the singing of songs smacked of the theater, and the theater was *tref*—unclean. In our home, the "world" itself was *tref*. Many years were to pass before I began to understand how much sense there was in this attitude.

But Krochmalna Street did not wish to take note of such thoughts. For Krochmalna Street, Purim was a grand carnival. The street was filled with maskers and bearers of gifts. It smelled of cinnamon, saffron and chocolate, of freshly-baked cakes and all sorts of sweets and spices whose names I did not know. The sweet-shops sold cookies in the shapes of King Ahasuerus, Haman the Wicked, the chamberlain Harbona, Queen Vashti, and Vaizatha, the tenth son of Haman. It was good to bite off Haman's leg, or to swallow the head of Queen Esther. And the noisemakers kept up a merry clamor, in defiance of all the Hamans of all the ages.

Among betrothed couples, and boys and girls who were "going with each other," the sending of Purim gifts was obligatory. This was part of the customary exchange of engagement presents. Because of one such Purim gift, an argument arose that almost led to a *Din Torah*, or rabbinical trial, in our house.

A young man sent his betrothed a silver box, but when she opened it—in the presence of her sister and her girl friends, who were impatiently awaiting the arrival of the gift—she found it contained a dead mouse! She uttered an unearthly shriek and fainted. The other girls screeched and screamed. After the bride-to-be had been revived with compresses of cold water and vinegar, and her friends had collected their wits, they began to plot revenge. The bride-to-be knew the reason for her boyfriend's outrageous deed. Several days before, they had quarreled. After much talk and discussion, the young women decided to repay the malicious youth in kind. Instead of a dead mouse, however, they sent him a fancy cake—filled with refuse. The baker was party to the conspiracy. The girls of Krochmalna Street looked upon this conflict as a war between the sexes, and Krochmalna Street had something to laugh about that Purim. The strange part of it was that the young man, although he had committed a revolting act, had not expected an equally odious retaliation, and was no less stunned than his fiancée had been. People quickly added imaginary incidents. The girls of Krochmalna Street always believed in laughing. One often heard bursts of uncontrolled laughter that might have come from an insane asylum. This time they chortled and chuckled from one end of the street to the other. The young man, too, had been surrounded by friends at the festive Purim meal. He, too, had been aided and abetted in his prank.

Yes, that Purim was a merry one. But the next morning everyone had sobered up and the warring clans came to us for a *Din Torah*. The room was jammed full with people. The bride-to-be had brought her family and her girl friends, and the groom was accompanied by his relatives and cronies. All of them were shouting as they climbed up the stairs, and they kept on shouting for half an hour or more, and my father had yet to learn who was the accuser, who the defendant and what the tumult was about. But while they were yelling, screaming, hurling insults and curses, Father quietly pored over one of his books. He knew that sooner or later they would grow calm. Jews, after all, are not bandits. In the meanwhile, before more time had been wasted, he wanted to know what Rabbi Samuel Eliezer Edels meant by the comment in his book, *The Maharsha:* "And one might also say. . . ."

I was present in the room and soon knew all about the affair. I listened attentively to every insult, every curse. There was quarreling and bickering, but every once in a while someone ventured a mild word or the suggestion that it was senseless to break off a match for such foolishness. Others, however, raked up the sins of the past. One minute their words were wild and coarse, but the next minute they had changed their tune and were full of friendship and courtesy. From early childhood on, I have noted that for most people there is only one small step between vulgarity and "refinement," between blows and kisses, between spitting at one's neighbor's face and showering him with kindness.

After they had finished shouting, and everyone had grown hoarse, someone at last related the entire story to my father. Father was shocked.

"Shame! How can anyone do such things? It is a violation of the law: 'Ye shall not make your souls abominable. . . .' "

Father immediately cited a number of Biblical verses and laws. First, it was impious; second, it was loathsome; third, such acts lead to anger, gossip, slander, discord, and what not. It was also dangerous, for the victim, overcome by nausea, might have become seriously ill. And the defilement of edibles, the food which God had created to still man's hunger and over which benedictions were to be recited, was in itself a sacrilege. Father recalled the sage who used to say that he merited long life if only because he had never left bread crumbs lying on the ground. He reminded them that, in order for a cake to be baked, someone had to till the soil and sow the grain, and then rain and dew had to fall from heaven. It was no small thing that out of a rotting seed in the earth a stalk of wheat burst forth. All the wise men of the world together could not create such a stalk. And here, instead of thanking and praising the Almighty for His bounty, men had taken this gift and used it to provoke their neighbors—had defiled what He had created.

Where formerly there had been an uproar, silence now reigned. The women wiped their eyes with their aprons. The men bowed their heads. The girls bashfully lowered their eyelids. After Father's words there was no more talk of a *Din Torah*. A sense of shame and solemnity seemed to have overcome everyone. Out of my father's mouth spoke the Torah, and all understood that every word was just. I was often to witness how my father, with his simple words, routed pettiness, vain ambition, foolish resentment, and conceit.

After Father's admonition the bride- and groom-to-be made peace. The mothers, who just a few minutes before had hurled insults at each other, now embraced. Talk of setting a date for the wedding was heard. My father received no fee, for there had been no actual *Din Torah*. His words of mild reproach had damaged his own livelihood. But no matter, for the weeks between Purim and Passover were a time of relative prosperity for us. Together with the Purim delicacies, the neighbors had sent a half ruble or a ruble each. And soon the pre-Passover sale of leavened bread would begin.

When the study had emptied, Father called me over and cautioned me to take heed of what may happen to those who do not study the Torah but concern themselves only with the vanities of this world.

The next Sabbath, after the *cholent*, the Sabbath stew, I went out on the balcony. The air was mild. The snow had long since melted. The pavements were dry. In the gutter flowed little streamlets whose ripples reflected the blue of the sky and the gold of the sun. The young couples of Krochmalna Street were starting out on their Sabbath walks. Suddenly the two who had sent each other the ugly gifts passed by. They walked arm in arm, chatting animatedly, smiling. A boy and his girl had quarreled—what of it?

I stood on the balcony in my satin gaberdine and my velvet hat, and gazed about me. How vast was this world, and how rich in all kinds of people and strange happenings! And how high was the sky above the rooftops! And how deep the earth beneath the flagstones! And why did men and women love each other? And where was God, who was constantly spoken of in our house? I was amazed, delighted, entranced. I felt that I must solve this riddle, I alone, with my own understanding.

From In My Father's Court,
translated by Channah Kleinerman-Goldstein,
Elaine Gottlieb, and Joseph Singer

ISAAC BASHEVIS SINGER

Reb Asher the Dairyman

Is it really true, as the author says in this story, that "there are some people in this world who are simply born good"? The mild and strong Reb Asher the Dairyman is such a man, a simple pious soul who befriended the author as a boy and allowed him to ride on his wagon all across Warsaw. Years later, remembering Reb Asher, the author sees him as typical of those Jews whom the Nazis sent to the death camp of Treblinka during the Second World War—Jews "who lived in sanctity and died as martyrs."

There are some people in this world who are simply born good. Such was Reb Asher the dairyman. God had endowed him with many, many gifts. He was tall, broad, strong, with a black beard, large black eyes, and the voice of a lion. On the New Year and the Day of Atonement he served as cantor of the main prayer for the congregation that met in our house, and it was his voice that attracted many of the worshipers. He did this without payment, although he could have commanded sizable fees from some of the larger synagogues. It was his way of helping my father earn a livelihood for the holidays. And as if this were not enough, Reb Asher was always doing something for us in one way or another. No one sent my father as generous a Purim gift as did Reb Asher the dairyman. When Father found himself in great straits and could not pay the rent, he sent me to Reb Asher to borrow the money. And Asher never said no, nor did he ever pull a wry face. He simply reached into his trouser pocket and pulled out a handful of paper money and silver. Neither did he limit himself to helping out my father. He gave charity in all directions. This simple Jew, who with great difficulty plowed through a chapter of the *Mishnah*, lived his entire life on the highest ethical plane. What others preached, he practiced.

He was no millionaire; he was not even wealthy, but he had a "comfortable income," as my father would put it. I myself often bought milk, butter, cheese, clabber, and cream in his shop. His wife and their eldest daughter waited on customers all day long, from early in the morning till late at night. His wife was a stout woman, with a blond wig, puffy cheeks, and a neck covered with freckles. She was the daughter of a farm bailiff. Her enormous bosom seemed to be swollen with milk. I used to imagine that if someone were to cut her arm, milk would spurt forth, and not blood. One son, Yudl, was so fat that people came to stare at him as at a freak. He weighed nearly three hundred and fifty pounds. Another son, slight of build and something of a dandy, had become a tailor and gone off to Paris. A younger son was still studying at the *heder* and a little girl attended a secular school.

Just as our house was always filled with problems, doubts, and unrest, so everything in Asher's house was whole, placid, healthy. Every day Asher went to bring the cans of milk from the train. He rose at the break of dawn, went to the synagogue, and then drove to the railroad depot. He worked at least eighteen hours every day; yet on the Sabbath, instead of resting, he would go to listen to a preacher or come to my father to study a portion of the Pentateuch with the commentary of Rashi. Just as he loved his work, so he loved his Judaism. It seems to me that I never heard this man say no. His entire life was one great yes.

Asher owned a horse and wagon, and this horse and wagon aroused a fierce envy in me. How happy must be the boy whose father owned a wagon, a horse, a stable! Every day Asher went off to distant parts of the city, even to Praga! Often I would see him driving past our house. He never forgot to lift his head and to greet whomever he saw at the window or on the balcony. Often he met me when I was running about the streets with a gang of boys or playing with those who were not "my kind," but he never threatened to tell my father, nor did he try to lecture me. He did not, like the other grownups, pull little boys by the ear, pinch their noses, or twist the brims of their caps. Asher seemed to have an innate respect for everyone, big or small.

Once when I saw him driving by in his wagon I nodded to him and called out: "Reb Asher, take me along!"

Asher immediately stopped and told me to get on. We drove to a train depot. The trip took several hours and I was overjoyed. I rode amid trolley cars, droshkies, loading vans. Soldiers marched; policemen stood

guard; fire engines, ambulances, even some of the auto-
mobiles that were just beginning to appear on the
streets of Warsaw rushed past us. Nothing could harm
me. I was protected by a friend with a whip, and beneath my feet I could feel the throbbing of the wheels.
It seemed to me that all Warsaw must envy me. And
indeed people stared in wonderment at the little Hasid
with the velvet cap and the red earlocks who was riding
in a milk wagon surveying the city. It was evident that
I did not really belong to this wagon, that I was a
strange kind of tourist. . . .

From that day on, a silent pact existed between
me and Reb Asher. Whenever he could, he would take
me along as his passenger. Fraught with danger were
those minutes when Reb Asher went off to fetch the
milk cans from a train, or to attend to a bill, and I
remained alone in the wagon. The horse would turn
his head and stare at me in astonishment. Asher had
given me the reins to hold, and the horse seemed to be
saying silently: "Just look who is my driver now. . . ."
The fear that the horse might suddenly rear up and
run off gave to these moments the extra fillip of peril.
After all, a horse is not a child's plaything but a gigantic
creature, silent, wild, with enormous strength. Occasionally a gentile would pass by, look at me, laugh,
and say something in Polish. I did not understand his
language, and he cast the same sort of dread upon me
as did the horse; he too was big, strong, and incompre-
hensible. He too might suddenly turn upon me and
strike me, or yank at my earlock—a pastime the Poles
considered a great joke. . . .

When I thought the end had come—any moment
now the gentile would strike me, or the horse would
dash off and smash into a wall or a street lamp—then

Reb Asher reappeared and all was well again. Asher carried the heavy milk cans with the ease of a Samson. He was stronger than the horse, stronger than the gentile, yet he had mild eyes and spoke my language, and he was my father's friend. I had only one desire: to ride with this man for days and nights over fields and through forests, to Africa, to America, to the ends of the world, and always to watch, to observe all that was going on around me. . . .

How different this same Asher appeared on the New Year and the Day of Atonement! Carpenters had put up benches in my father's study, and this was where the women prayed. The beds had been taken out of the bedroom, a Holy Ark brought in, and it had become a tiny prayer house. Asher was dressed in a white robe, against which his black beard appeared even blacker. On his head he wore a high cap embroidered with gold and silver. At the beginning of the Additional Service, Reb Asher would ascend to the cantor's desk and call out with the roaring of a lion: "Behold me, destitute of good works. . . ."

Our bedroom was too small for the bass voice that thundered forth from this mighty breast. It was heard halfway down the street. Asher recited and chanted. He knew every melody, every movement. The twenty men who made up our congregation were all part of his choir. Asher's deep masculine voice aroused a tumult in the women's section. True, they all knew him well. Only yesterday they had bought from him or from his wife a saucepan of milk, a pot of clabber, a few ounces of butter, and had bargained with him for a little extra. But now Asher was the delegate who offered up the prayers of the People of Israel directly to the Almighty, before the Throne of Glory, amid fluttering angels and books that read themselves, in which are recorded the good deeds and the sins of every mortal soul. . . . When he reached the prayer "We will express the might," and began to recite the destinies of men—who shall live and who shall die, who shall perish by fire and who by water—a sobbing broke out among the women. But when Asher called out triumphantly: "But repentance, prayer, and charity can avert the evil decree!"—then a heavy stone was taken from every heart. Soon Asher began to sing of the smallness of man and the greatness of God, and joy and comfort enveloped everyone. Why need men—who are but passing shadows, wilting blossoms—expect malice from a God who is just, revered, merciful? Every word that Asher called out, every note he uttered restored courage, revived hope. We indeed are nothing, but He is all. We are but as dust in our lifetime, and less than dust after death, but He is eternal and His days shall never end. In Him, only in Him, lies our hope. . . .

One year, at the close of the Day of Atonement, this same Asher, our friend and benefactor, saved our very lives. It happened in this manner. After the day-long fast, we had eaten the repast. Later a number of Jews gathered in our house to dance and rejoice. My father had already put up the first beam of the hut for the coming Festival of Tabernacles. Late that night we had at last fallen asleep. Since benches and pews had been set up in the bedroom, and the entire house was in disorder, each of us slept wherever he could find a spot. But one thing we had forgotten—to extinguish the candles that were still burning on some of the pews.

Late that night Asher had to drive to the railroad station to pick up milk. He passed our house and

noticed that it was unusually bright. This was not the
glow of candles, or of a lamp, but rather the glare of a
great fire. Asher realized that our house must be burning. He rang the bell at the gate, but the janitor did
not rush to open it. He too was asleep. Then Asher set
to ringing the bell and beating on the door with such a
furor that at last the gentile awoke and opened the
gate. Asher raced up the stairs and knocked on our
door, but no one answered. Then Asher the mighty
hurled his broad shoulders against the door and forced
it open. Bursting into the house, he found the entire
family asleep while all around, benches, prayer stands,
prayer books, and holiday prayer books were aflame.
He began to call out in his booming cantorial voice and
finally roused us, and then he tore off our quilts and
set to smothering the conflagration.

I remember that moment as though it had been
yesterday. I opened my eyes and saw many flames, large
and small, rolling about and dancing like imps. My
brother Moishe's blanket had already caught fire. But
I was very young and was not frightened. On the con-
trary, I liked the dancing flames.

After some time the fire was put out. Here indeed
something had happened that might well be called a
miracle. A few minutes more, and we would all have
been enveloped by the flames, for the wood of the
benches was dry and they were saturated with the
tallow of the dripping candles. Asher was the only
human being who was awake at that hour and who was
prepared to be so persistent with the ringing of the bell
and who would risk his own life for us. Yes, it was fated
that this faithful friend should save us from an infernal
fire.

We were not even able to thank him. It was as

though we had all been struck dumb. Asher himself was in a hurry and left quickly. We wandered about amid the charred benches, tables, prayer books, and prayer shawls, and every few minutes we discovered more sparks and smoldering embers. We might all easily have been burnt to cinders.

The friendship between my father and Reb Asher grew ever stronger, and during the war years, when we were close to starvation, Asher again helped us in every way he could.

After we had left Warsaw (during the First World War), we continued to hear news of him from time to time. One son died, a daughter fell in love with a young man of low origins and Asher was deeply grieved. I do not know whether he lived to see the Nazi occupation of Warsaw. He probably died before that. But such Jews as he were dragged off to Treblinka. May these memoirs serve as a monument to him and his like, who lived in sanctity and died as martyrs.

From In My Father's Court,
translated by Channah Kleinerman-Goldstein,
Elaine Gottlieb, and Joseph Singer

ITZIK MANGER

The Adventures of Hershel Summerwind

Don't think that because Jewish life in the old country was hard, there were no pleasures, no carefree moments, no abandonments to fantasy. Of course there were; all peoples find a few moments in their lives for play. Here is Hershel Summerwind, a Jewish scamp who gets into many scrapes, but somehow, perhaps because of his good nature and perhaps because of God's mercy, always manages to get out with a whole skin and a merry smile. This story tells of his madcap flight with a horde of drunken birds.

It was years ago. Hershel was a youth of eighteen or nineteen, the picture of health. His younger sister Eidel had already married, but the stepmother continued to grumble, "In some families such a boy is already a father, but this one hangs around, idle and empty-handed, chasing the girls. You'll have the same end as my Mendel, mark my words!"

But who cares if a stepmother grumbles? She had never been a friend of his, and since Mendel the rooster died—even less of a friend!

Incidentally, every year on the day of Mendel's death she donates candles for the synagogue and hires Oyzer the *shammes* to say *Kaddish*.

In short, Hershel's younger sister Eidel was happily married and within the year had a son. Two days before the circumcision Hershel's father called him aside and said, "Harness the horse, my son, and ride to Daraban. Tell Zalman the innkeeper to give you a barrel of wine he put aside for me twenty years ago. And with God's help, tell him, the day after tomorrow will be the happiest day of my life—the first grandchild! Take the whip, harness the horse, and come back quickly with the barrel of wine, so we can carry off the circumcision in grand style."

Twenty years ago when Hershel's father and Zalman the innkeeper had met after a long separation— they were old pals, one body, one soul!—Zalman had lowered a barrel of wine into the cellar, and, clapping his friend on the back, had told him that the wine would be his when the happiest day of his life arrived. And for almost twenty years the barrel of wine had been waiting in Zalman's cellar.

Hershel hitched up the horse and wagon, took the whip with the red handle, and sang out, "Giddap, Brownie, we're off to Daraban!"

The road to Daraban was long—uphill and downhill, fields and woods, trees along the way, birds and golden sun. The horse trotted quickly, not waiting for Hershel to prod him with the whip.

Hershel felt gay. He flourished his whip in the air. On his lips danced a rhyme:

"We speed along to Daraban,
We speed along our joyous trip,
Says the horse, 'Don't spur me on.
Hershel, throw away your whip.'"

Hershel felt the whip was useless—that's why he
made up the rhyme. Perhaps, too, because with a
rhyme it's less lonely on the road.

That night when Hershel arrived at Daraban, Zalman the innkeeper was overjoyed to see him—no small
thing, the only son of his oldest friend. He slapped
Hershel on the back. "How's your father? Getting on,
eh?"

And when Hershel told him his mission, Zalman
slapped his back again. "That means we have to celebrate. You may be sure the barrel is waiting. With the
years it's become better." Sighing, he said, "Ah, if only
man were like a barrel of wine."

Hershel unharnessed the horse. He had brought a
sack of oats from home, but Zalman would not let him
open it. "You'll use your sack on the way home. Today
your colt is the guest of my colt. They'll eat from the
same trough. My colt likes having guests. Takes after
his master. Understand, Hershel?"

Zalman the innkeeper invited Hershel into the
dining room, poured out two glasses of wine, and said,
"Long life, Hershel, and may your father have joy of
you."

Hershel was tired and hungry from the long trip.
Noticing this, Zalman cried, "You're hungry, Hershel!
My old lady should be back any minute—she went to
a funeral."

Hershel knew that Zalman's wife, Ziessel, never
missed a funeral. Coming home from a funeral she

would always say, "May all Jewish children enjoy such
a funeral." That's why she was nicknamed "Ziessel-
may-all-Jewish-children."

As soon as Ziessel came home she immediately began to prepare dinner, saving her account of the funeral for later. But once everyone was at the table she
could no longer restrain herself and began, "May all
Jewish children enjoy such a funeral. . . ."

Hershel didn't relish his food. Wearily he fell upon
his bed, and in his dream he saw a funeral. Four Jews
carry a coffin. The father follows, downcast. Sighing,
he says to the stepmother, "No more Hershel!" The
stepmother gibes, "Some bargain, your Hershel . . ."
Suddenly, as if from the earth, Ziessel the innkeeper's
wife appears. She points to the coffin. She shouts at the
top of her voice, "Such a funeral our Hershel had, may
all Jewish children enjoy such a funeral."

The funeral vanishes. It never happened, it's really
a circumcision—Hershel's circumcision. Everyone joins
in the ceremony. They drink wine, eat cake. Hershel
sees Itche the circumciser, a knife between his teeth,
prepare for the ritual. Hershel wants to cry out that
he's already been circumcised, but he can't. He wants
to run away, but his feet are heavy as lead.

Hershel woke up and spat three times to ward off
the evil eye. In the street people were already at work.
Peasants were sitting in the inn drinking wine and
smoking *mahorka*. Quick as a flash, Hershel dressed
himself, said his prayers on the run, and hitched up his
horse. Zalman the innkeeper helped him lift the barrel
of wine onto the wagon, then sang out, "Giddap,
Brownie!"

Only after he had left Daraban did the shadow

of last night's dream disappear. Here was the windmill, here he turned to the open road—uphill, downhill, through fields and woods, all the way home. The whip was again unnecessary, but, having brought it, Hershel carried it back.

It was a hot summer day. The road was dusty. Hershel took off his jacket. "Ah, a pleasure." But the farther he went, the more the sun burned. His throat became so dry he could hardly catch his breath. Suddenly it occurred to him that he was indeed a fool: in the wagon lay a barrel of wine, while he was expiring from thirst. True, it was for the circumcision, but what would be the harm in taking a sip and slaking his thirst? And without a second thought Hershel pulled the cork out of the barrel, bent down, and took a good long drink.

The wine was old and rich. After one gulp Hershel's head began to swim; his eyes began to close; and he was soon asleep.

How long he slept there Hershel Summerwind does not remember, but when he awoke he saw a strange picture indeed: scattered around the wagon lay more than a hundred birds, all dead drunk.

Only then did Hershel remember that he had forgotten to cork the barrel. While he slept the birds must have gathered, sipped the wine, and fallen to the earth, drunk.

Hershel sprang down from the wagon, afraid the birds would fly away once they became sober. A shame —so many beautiful birds. It will be a real celebration when they start singing tomorrow at the circumcision.

Hershel found a thread in his pocket, and one by one he bound the little feet of the birds, who were still soundly sleeping. When he had finished binding their feet, he wound the thread around his belly and made a strong knot. Now they wouldn't be able to fly away even when they became sober. Hershel Summerwind, pleased with this piece of work, took another good long drink from the barrel of wine and again fell fast asleep.

When he woke, his feet were fluttering through the air and his head was touching the clouds.

While he had been sleeping so soundly, the birds had sobered up, shaken the sleep from their wings, and flown off with Hershel Summerwind—up, up, to the clouds that were sailing through the sky.

Hershel's heart pounded with fear. Below, his horse was neighing. It called to him, reminded him that the wine was unprotected, that tomorrow was the circumcision; his father's feast would be spoiled.

"A pretty story," Hershel reproached himself. "What did you need birds for, eh? Now you're in for it, Hershel Summerwind. They're carrying you off the way the devil carries a thief. And who knows where they'll take you?"

But his reproaches didn't help. It was too late.

Hershel shouted down to the horse, which stood patiently in the middle of the road, not knowing what to do. "Take home the barrel of wine, Brownie! You know the way. Farewell, Brownie, and regards to my father. A *mazel tov* to my sister, and a fig to my stepmother!"

The horse lifted its ears, to make out what Hershel was shouting from the clouds. He must have understood, for he soon began to pull the wagon and started off without master or whip.

The birds that were carrying our Hershel higher

and higher burst into song. A delightful melody, a song
sweeter than all songs, a song for the sun, for the
winds and the clouds. Hershel listened to the song for
a while and then joined in himself. His voice was a
good one. The birds were astonished and talked it over
among themselves.

"It's a strange bird that flies with us, but he certainly can sing."

"Of course it's a strange bird," called out another,
"and his song is entirely different. Reminds me of ripe
red cherries."

"Red cherries," chimed in a youngish bird. "I love
red cherries."

"Listen to the wizard," jeered a middle-aged bird.
"Who doesn't like to pick cherries? Only a fool."

"Know what, fellows?" said an elderly bird. "Let's
fly to Zeinvel's orchard—the cherries must be ripe by
now."

"To the cherry orchard! To the cherry orchard,"
piped all the birds and quickly took off for Tziganesht,
where Zeinvel's orchard lay.

The birds, Hershel tells us, made a mess of the
orchard. The scarecrows were helpless.

But thanks to this flight Hershel's life was saved.
The flying frightened him, his head grew dizzy, his
eyes teared, his ears were humming. But as soon as the
birds descended to the first cherry tree, Hershel cut the
thread in half and sprang down from the tree, jumped
over the fence, and set off for home. It was only four
miles. He ran without stopping to catch his breath, and
after the evening prayers were done he staggered, half
alive, into his father's house. The horse was already
waiting there, in front of the door, with the barrel of

wine—so no one guessed what had befallen our Hershel.

The next day, at the circumcision, Hershel told the story of the birds and the great miracle that had followed. And so that all should know he was telling the truth Hershel Summerwind sang the song the birds had sung when they carried him through the air.

From this story you can see what a great and good God we have. For if He helped such an idler as Hershel Summerwind, He will certainly help all faithful and God-fearing Jews, who follow His commandment and live by His word.

translated by Irving Howe

JOSEPH OPATOSHU

————•⟨∞⟩•————

The Machine

*This simple little sketch captures a moment in the ex-
perience of immigrant Jews in America during the early
years of the century. Most of them had to go to work
in factories and shops to feed their families. They
worked terribly long hours for very low wages, until
they finally organized themselves to improve their conditions. In this story, which shows the immigrant
workers at an early stage, before they gained the con-
fidence to defend themselves, their fears and anxieties
are portrayed with a quiet sympathy.*

————•⟨∞⟩•————

Brodsky's shoe factory in New York was all astir.
Workers were up in arms, calling for a strike so that
dozens of families wouldn't be left without an income.
Everyone was talking about the new machine, which
was expected any day now and could supposedly stitch
thirty soles in an hour.

Only the Sephardic Jews (those who came from
around the Mediterranean) didn't take part in the hub-

bub. They were absolutely dumbstruck by the news
and unable to cooperate with their brothers, the Ashkenazi Jews (from eastern Europe). Their thin faces became gloomier, their soft, heart-felt singing had
stopped, and their black, dreamy eyes grew eloquent,
pleading: "Don't throw us out, don't take the bread
from the mouths of so many families."

The Ashkenazi sole-stitchers gradually left the
factory rather than wait for the machine to shove them
out, and only the Sephardic Jews remained. Now was
their chance. They came in earlier than usual and
stayed into the night, realizing they had to benefit from
the extra piecework because today or tomorrow everybody would be laid off.

They sat there silently, barely exchanging a word,
and whenever the foreman or the boss came by, their
eyes grew humble as though asking him not to bully
them—they were having a hard enough time working
and they weren't in anyone's way.

A young Sephardi with a moustache was unable
to stay put. He had been walking around crushed ever
since he had found out that a stitching-machine was
coming. He had postponed his wedding for a month,
and now a whole week had gone by, and he still didn't
know what to do.

"It's a bad thing, Rakhimi," he said to his neighbor.

"You mean about the machine?" said the other
man, who was working with two lengths of shoemaker's
thread. "Yes, it's really a bad thing."

"If I hadn't put off my wedding, I wouldn't care."
The young Sephardi kept raising his long hands.

"Stop worrying, don't take it to heart!" his neighbor comforted him. "There's no machine coming in as

yet! The Ashkenazis got scared and took off, and there's new work arriving all the time. So why worry!"

The foreman came by and counted up the completed shoes. The young Sephardi gathered his courage and asked:

"When's the machine coming in?"

"You looking forward to it?" the foreman smiled.

"I hope it falls apart on the way over!" the neighbor threw in.

"I hope it sinks into the ground."

"Amen!" several others chimed in.

The foreman smiled and reassured them:

"Maybe they won't bring it! Just keep working! We've got to send out the entire lot today! Get going!"

A week or two went by, and they forgot all about the machine. No one in the factory spoke about it any more. And the work moved at a furious clip. They were advertising for more workers, and wages were going up.

The gloomy faces of the Sephardim began to brighten, their terror at losing their jobs melted away, and the young Sephardi set a date for his wedding. He was no longer frightened of the foreman, and even joked:

"Are they bringing in a machine?"

"They sure are!" said the foreman irritably, but no one believed him.

Some twenty pairs of hands drew the threads, went up and down, as though conducting the hubbub in the factory. One worker burst into a chant. The others joined in, and the whole factory was filled with a soft, melancholy crooning, just as in earlier days.

Working from dawn to night, the Sephardim felt at ease, cheerful, and certain that no one was thinking about the machine any more. The young Sephardi, who was getting ready for his wedding, said to his neighbor:

"Good thing we didn't walk out!"

"How can anyone listen to those Ashkenazis. They're a bunch of hare-brained socialists!" the neighbor burst out. "They think the boss ought to cut them in and give them his fortune. If they hadn't left, they could still be working now! A couple of lots of material came in again today. There hasn't been a season like this for a long time!"

Week after week went by, and as the work kept up at its furious clip, one man brought in a relative, another a neighbor, and in a short while half of Salonika's Sephardim was in the factory, crooning old Jewish chants and Sabbath hymns into the American soles.

One Sunday morning, when columns of leather dust were hovering at the windows, dozens of hands were going up and down, and a soft chant was weaving through the hubbub, a mysterious hand flung heavy ropes across the windows, and a shudder went through the factory.

"What's that?" the young Sephardi called out.

"Trouble!"

"They're gonna paint the building," someone threw in.

"Really?" said several men in relief.

Then they heard a scraping. A man removed a window, he signaled with his hands, and the ropes began to groan.

The young Sephardi couldn't stay seated. He hurried over to the window, looked down, saw the machine coming up, and turned pale.

Everyone was looking at him, waiting for him to say something. He shook his head as though smiling, and sat down again.

The workers became strangely quiet. Their hands stopped going up and down. Their eyes were riveted on the window, where a machine, black and massive, peered in, flapped its wings over the Sephardim, and came swooping down upon them.

translated by Joachim Neugroschel

ISAIAH SPIEGEL

Blossoms

*The outer events of this story are sparse and quiet: a
Jewish boy's yearning for some blossoms as he is
trapped in the Warsaw Ghetto during the Second
World War, and a gentile boy's offer to give him some.
But behind the surface we can detect the most terrible
event in all Jewish history, the destruction of millions
of Jews by Hitler during these years.*

When Mendele climbed onto the roof of their small
wooden house for the first time, he saw a yard filled
with the broken chimneys of houses that had been
leveled to the ground. No trace of a fence or boundary
remained; all the yards in the Warsaw ghetto had become one big open space.

While his mother was away at work, Mendele
would spend his time wandering among the shell-holes
—piles of broken glass and twisted iron. And now as he
stood there on the roof, the stones and piles of junk
suddenly struck him as very queer. All the more so
since, when he looked across the fences that lay beyond

the ghetto, and across the barbed wire that ran close
to their own house, what he saw made him open his
eyes with amazement. He simply could not understand
how all this had happened without his knowledge.
Shielding his eyes against the sun, he stood on tiptoe,
motionless, frozen to the spot. He strained his eyes
until they filled with tears. He remained standing there
until a high-pitched voice called out to him from the
direction where Jews couldn't live:

"Hey you! Jew boy, hey!"

Mendele looked around but could see no one. There
wasn't a soul to be seen. Everyone in the ghetto was
at work. Directly across from him on the gentile side
there was a meager little garden where a few trees were
starting to bloom. The smallest ones were dressed in
little white shirts made entirely of bloom. They were
cherry trees. Mendele could not have enough of looking at them. In all his life he had never seen such a
beautiful garden. Wherever his eye fell it met with
white and green, green and white. The peaceful ground
was covered with fresh grasses, while the silvery-white
trees with their accents of rosy-red looked as if little
lanterns were being lit among them.

At first Mendele couldn't remember when and
where he had seen such beauty. It must have been very
long ago, before the war, when they hadn't lived in the
ghetto. It must have been in his Uncle Michael's orchard, before the Germans had taken his father away.
They had taken him in the morning, just as he stood
there in the middle of his prayers. Mendele remembered that in his Uncle Michael's orchards there had
also been trees like the ones across the way, but bigger.
There were apple trees and plum trees, and also a huge
old pear tree covered with small green fruit. At his

Uncle Michael's there were even gooseberries that grew on thorny bushes. What hadn't there been in his Uncle Michael's orchard!

Looking around the ghetto yards, Mendele sees that there are no trees anywhere, except beside one little house there is a skinny crippled tree which stares at the sky like an old broom. Last winter all the trees in the ghetto were chopped down, and for a long time they lay stretched out across the streets like corpses. The wood from those trees went into the ghetto kitchens —so his mother told him—because there was no other fuel. One sawed-off tree, not far from their door, even began to sprout little green buds. But now there isn't a speck of green in the Jewish yards, while across the barbed wire there's a whole festival of growth.

Mendele looks toward the gentile garden and sees that it is green all over. The grass snuggles up to the earth, and even the trees look as if they were dressed up for a wedding. The smell of new plants hangs in the air. And now Mendele hears again the voice calling to him from across the barbed wire:

"Hey there, Jew boy!"

Mendele looks but can't see anyone. There isn't a soul in the ghetto yard either. His mother and the two youths who live in their yard have all gone off to work. The mysterious voice must be calling from across the fence where the trees are.

Who can be calling him? The owner of the voice is surely hiding someplace. Then Mendele sees one of the branches bending on the trees across the fence, and from among its blossoms a face looks out at him, and the face has its mouth open, and its tongue stuck out and is calling:

"Jew boy, Jew boy!"

Mendele knows that Jews don't live across the wire, and that the people who do live there don't wear yellow patches sewn to their clothes. Across the wire the gentiles live in a world which isn't fenced in. His mother refers to them every now and again. In that world you can get everything, and you can walk wherever you want to, on whichever street you like, and sometimes you can even hear a harmonica playing from an open window. You can hear people laughing. More than once it had happened that, when he was lying on his straw mat in the corner and couldn't get to sleep because of hunger, he heard distant songs and melodies floating across as if a violin were crying somewhere in the night. Occasionally it happened also that the doves flew into the ghetto from across the fences and stood on the roofs here—velvety doves of greenish white and gun metal. Once one of these doves almost flew into their house, and another time a cat crossed the barbed wire and lay for a few days beside their chimney. The cat cried at night just like a baby, and his mother cursed bitterly because of her lost sleep.

But Mendele had made friends with the cat. In the daytime he had stood underneath the roof and thrown up a ball of wool to the cat until his mother had run out and screamed at him to stop.

To Mendele it seemed as if that cat was not really a cat at all, but a lost soul, maybe a Jew who had sinned and was expiating his sin in the shape of a cat. All this flashed through Mendele's mind in the same instant that he saw the face with its tongue stuck out moving among the blossoms.

Mendele takes a piece of broken mirror out of his pocket and catches the light of the sun so that it will blind the face in the tree across the barbed wire. He

likes to send these bright rays of sun flying, and now
the piece of broken glass aims a silver band of light
across the yard and strikes the face across the barbed
wire. The face blinks its eyes; it doesn't like the sun
shining into them. The boy climbs out of the tree and
stands barefoot on the ground below. Then he runs to
the fence, climbs onto it, so that he and Mendele are
sitting opposite each other. Between them is barbed
wire and a narrow cobbled street. At the end of the
cobbled street you can just glimpse the dark red kiosk
of the German guard.

The two boys sit opposite each other in silence. For
the first time they see each other close up. They don't
utter a word. Mendele is afraid that his mother might
catch and punish him. Still, he wants very much to have
one of the branches of the blossoming tree. He would
be satisfied with just one little branch and he would
plant it in the yard outside his window. Maybe it would
send out a little shoot in time for *Shevuoth*. But how
can he say this to the boy on the other side of the barbed
wire? Mendele makes signs to the boy and points to the
trees in the other's garden.

"You want some?" calls the boy, pointing to the
blossoming trees.

"Yes, yes, I want a branch, a green one," Mendele
nods, "a little one, just a tiny one."

The other boy leaps from the fence and runs towards the trees. Mendele's heart begins to flutter. He
trembles with expectation and prays that nothing should
interfere. He sees how the other one is now standing
close to the tree and is bending one of its white
branches.

Just then someone grabs Mendele from behind so
he almost loses his breath.

His mother stands there angry and distracted: "Heaven help me! Get off the roof or you'll be the death of us all."

Mendele doesn't know how to get down. It looks as if he's going to fall directly into his mother's hands and get a beating.

He lets himself down very slowly at first, and then jumps, tearing the sleeve of his jacket. His mother catches him and slaps him about.

"You bandit you! Isn't it enough that I'm a widow? Must I also raise a son who is a devil?"

She drags him into the house and the sounds of Mendele's crying can be heard for a long time.

Mendele doesn't fall alseep so fast. His mother's slaps are still burning his face. When at last he does fall alseep, he has a beautiful dream. . . . He is walking with his mother in Uncle Michael's orchard. It is late summer. The trees are heavy with bright fruits. Huge plums as big as your fist hang from the branches; apples and pears lie scattered through the high grasses. Uncle Michael, a tall skinny Jew in a long coat, bids him climb a tree and pick cherries. Mendele just barely manages to climb a cherry tree, and remains sitting on one of the branches that is laden with ruby-red and yellowish-white cherries. First he picks and throws the cherries down into a woven straw basket; then he picks them for himself and puts the cherries into his mouth. They are sweet, and the juice runs down his lips. He sits there hidden in the branches of the cherry tree. His mother stands underneath and looks up smilingly, and beside her is his Uncle Michael. As Mendele throws cherries into the basket, his mother and his uncle keep emptying it. Mendele picks almost half the cherries from the cherry tree and then, when he tries to move

to another branch, he suddenly sees sitting not far
from him a second boy who is also picking cherries.

He can't remember where he has seen that boy
before. He knows he's seen those eyes somewhere. The
other boy is leaning toward him and whispering so that
Uncle Michael and his mother can't hear.

"Yes, I want them, I do want them," answers
Mendele, shaking the branch he's sitting on. It feels
as if it's going to fall and break any minute and he,
Mendele will fall too, deep, deep down. And now he
feels he is actually falling. He falls and falls, and as he
falls he is being covered with cherries, with leaves, with
branches. He sinks deeper and ever deeper into an
empty well. . . .

When Mendele opens his eyes at dawn it is still
dark in the house. A skimpy bit of light from a desolate
sun filters in through a crack in the wall. Mendele wakes
up to find his mother standing over him scolding; "Small
wonder that you cry out in your sleep, hankering after
gentile cats and playmates. May the Lord send such
bitter nightmares to each of our enemies!"

Mendele can't bring himself to open his eyes. In
the country of his sleep Uncle Michael's orchard is still
blossoming and he can't understand why his mother
should be scolding him so early in the morning. A flock
of summery mirror-birds comes showering down over
his bed from the crumbling ghetto sun outside. Mendele
still can't open his eyes. Over his face there hovers a
cool little cloud of air, fresh as the early morning mist
that hangs over the blossoming orchards.

translated by Miriam Waddington

About the Authors

SHOLOM ALEICHEM (*1859–1916*) is the greatest of all Yiddish writers. His real name was Sholom Rabinowitz, but he used as his pen name, Sholom Aleichem, which means "Peace Unto You" in Hebrew, the phrase with which Jews have traditionally greeted one another. Born in Russia, he tried for a time to earn his living as a businessman, but then devoted himself entirely to writing. He spent his final years in the United States, writing plays for the Yiddish stage and stories for the Yiddish press.

In his humorous stories, which often have an undercurrent of sadness, Sholom Aleichem touched the deepest emotions of Jewish life. His great characters, Tevye the dairyman and Menachem Mendl, represent the two extremes of Jewish outlook: simple moral strength and complicated day-dreaming. Sholom Aleichem also wrote some splendid stories for young people, which no one is too old to enjoy.

I. D. BERKOWITZ (*1885–1967*) was born in Russia, received a traditional Jewish education, and in his youth began to write in both Hebrew and Yiddish. He married a daughter of Sholom Aleichem, and in 1914 came to New York City together with the family of Sholom Aleichem. In later years he settled in Israel, where he became a distinguished Hebrew writer.

ITZIK MANGER (*1901–1969*), born in Rumania, is known to Yiddish readers primarily for his brilliant poetry. After the rise of Nazism, he led the life of a wanderer, moving about on the European continent and then settling in New York. Among his best poems are ballads that retell Biblical stories with humor and light-heartedness. He is probably the most carefree in spirit of the Yiddish writers included in this book.

ISAAC METZKER (*1901–   *), born in eastern Galicia, came to the United States at the age of 23. He lives in New York City and for many years has been a writer for the Yiddish newspaper, the *Jewish Daily Forward*. He is one of the few Yiddish writers to pay much attention to the life of Jewish farmers in eastern Europe.

JOSEPH OPATOSHU (*1887–1954*) received a traditional Jewish education while growing up in Poland. In 1907 he emigrated to the United States and seven years later received a degree in engineering. But his career as a writer soon absorbed all his energies. His fiction is notable for turning to subjects and characters neglected in earlier Yiddish writing: Jewish smugglers, horse thieves, unlettered toughs, and other vigorous, if unsavory, types.

I. L. PERETZ (*1851–1915*) was one of the founders of modern Yiddish literature. Born in Poland, he drifted for a time from one occupation to another, first as businessman and then as lawyer. In the 1880s he settled in Warsaw, where he became an official of the large Jewish community. For the rest of his life he remained active in Jewish affairs, touring the provinces of Russia and Poland to collect statistics about Jewish social life, participating briefly in the Jewish socialist movement, and serving as editor of the *Yiddishe Bibliotek,* an annual collection of literary and educational writings.

Though he began by composing satiric and realistic sketches, Peretz reached his greatest achievement in stories that are drawn from old Yiddish folktakes, especially those about the Hasidic rabbis. He retells these folktales in his own, modern, half-ironic way, thereby blending past and present, traditional piety and modern skepticism.

ABRAHAM REISEN (*1876–1953*), born in Russia, came from a cultivated Jewish family. Early in life he identified himself with the Jewish socialist movement and many of his stories and poems sound a note of gentle protest. He came to America in the early 1900s and lived here for the rest of his life. Reisen's hundreds of stories are notable for their humaneness of voice, a fragile delicacy of tone. In drawing the life of the Jews, he uses a light pencil, preferring to hint rather than stress.

ISAAC BASHEVIS SINGER (*1904–*) was born in Poland, received an orthodox Jewish education, and in 1926 became a journalist for the Yiddish press in Warsaw. Much influenced by his older brother, the gifted Yiddish novelist Israel Joshua Singer, he decided early in life to become a writer. He published a number of Yiddish novels while living in Poland; the best of these—*The Family Moskat* and *Satan in Goray*—can now be read in English translation. In 1935 Singer came to New York, joining the staff of the Yiddish daily newspaper, *The Forward,* for which he still writes regularly. His books were translated into English during recent years, and he has become one of the most admired writers of our time.

Glossary

Note: the *kh* sound in the transliteration of Yiddish and Hebrew words is pronounced as a guttural, in the back of one's throat.

Bar Mitzvah (bar-mìts-vah)—ceremony celebrating the thirteenth birthday of a Jewish boy, the point when he is traditionally supposed to assume religious responsibilities.

challah (khàl-leh *or* hàl-leh)—a twisted white bread used for the Sabbath.

cholent (chò-lent)—a Jewish dish, often served as a dessert, made of fruits or vegetables.

Din Torah (din tò-rah)—a rabbinical trial or court.

diaspora (die-às-po-rah)—state of exile, the condition of the Jews after dispersion from Palestine.

dreidl (drài-dl)—a top that Jewish children play with, especially at Hanukah time.

Elul (èl-ul)—the last month of the year in the Jewish calendar, usually coinciding with August.

gefilte fish (ge-fìl-te)—a dish of chopped fish, usually carp, used for the Sabbath.

Gemarah (ge-màh-rah)—a section of the Talmud.

goyisher kop (gòi-ish-er kòp)—a Yiddish phrase meaning, literally, "gentile head," used to suggest something less than brilliance of mind.

Haggadah (ha-gà-dah)—prayers and songs recited on the first two nights of the Passover holiday.

Haman (hàh-man)—an evil Persian official who sought the destruction of the Jews and was hanged when his plot was exposed to King Ahasuerus by Queen Esther; this event is celebrated by the Jewish holiday of Purim.

heder (hài-der)—Hebrew school.

Hanukah (hà-nook-ah)—a Jewish holiday commemorating the rededication of the Temple in Jerusalem by Judas Maccabeus in 165 B.C.

kaddish (kàh-dish)—mourner's prayer for a deceased close relative, usually said by the son.

kosher (kòh-sher)—preparation of food according to Jewish ritual.

knishes (knìsh-es)—a pastry made with fine dough and filled with potatoes, meat, or buckwheat.

mahorka (mah-hòr-kah)—a crude tobacco smoked by Russian peasants.

mazel tov (màh-zel tov)—congratulations, good luck.

menorah (men-ò-rah)—candelabrum used for religious purposes.

minyan (mìn-yan)—a quorum of ten males for religious services.

Mishnah (mìsh-nah)—the oral Jewish law which forms the basis of the Talmud.

Passover (pàss-over)—a Jewish holiday occurring in the spring of each year which celebrates the deliverance of the ancient Hebrews from slavery in Egypt.

Prophet Elijah—Old Testament prophet, believed in Jewish folklore to be the special friend of the poor.

Pentateuch (pèn-tah-tyook)—first five books of the Old Testament.

seder (sài-der)—the feast commemorating the Exodus of

the Jews from Egypt, observed on the first two days of
Passover.

shammes (shàm-mes)—sexton.

Shevuoth (shev-ù-oth)—Feast of the Pentecost, the holiday
commemorating the giving of the Torah to Moses.

shochet (shò-khet)—ritual slaughterer who prepares meat
that will be kosher.

shofar (shòw-far) ram's horn blown on High Holidays.

Succoth (sùk-oth)—Feast of the Booths, the fall harvest
holiday.

Talmud (tàl-mud)—collection of writings constituting traditional Jewish civil and religious law.

Torah (tòh-rah)—Old Testament.